# TIME BOMB

by

Mark J. Wilson

Based on a Short Story by

Mark J. Wilson and Linda Hazelwood

First Printing, 2020

ISBN: 978-1-63625-410-4

markjwilson.author@gmail.com

– — To my LUCKY —–

What if you worked with a homicidal maniac?

What if no one listened to your warnings?

What if you risked everything by bringing a stolen gun
to work for protection?

What if your girlfriend thought that YOU were the crazy one?

— —— ———————————————————————— —— —

"We are all born alone and we all die alone
and everyone we meet along the way
are merely acquaintances."

G. W. Bond

# MONDAY

*MARK J. WILSON*

"Layoffs? Here?... Where'd you hear this?" asked thirty-five year old, lighthearted jokester, Don Thorp to his friend that was on the phone. Don was a computer draftsman for Hunter Engineering, one of many large industrial corporations that resided in Ventura, California. Don was blond with piercing blue eyes, very good looking and was a friend to all, or, *almost* all.

"Layoffs," he heard. A word that can chill instantly when it's applied to you. Don sat up in his chair and asked, "When?" Yes, when? But the person didn't know. Only that it was, "In the works." Don said, "Well, hey, thanks for the call—and the warning... Yeah... Good luck," said Don in parting, "...'Bye." Don hung up and had a very troubled look about him. Yes, he was troubled about the layoffs, but even more so, because of the homicidal, walking "Time Bomb" of a coworker he had in another department of the same building at the same company.

Don sat in his office on the first floor in front of his computer drafting station. He stared at that very device from which he derived his livelihood and wondered, how much longer that would be the case. *Time to update my resume,* he thought and post it somewhere on one of those job posting sites.

But then, all of that paled in comparison to the thought of "Scary Larry" Jenkins going on a rampage of death—something that wouldn't be too far from an expected outcome, especially if he was terminated———And he would be. No question about it if layoffs happen———And they would. If you're going to downsize your company, the first thing you do is get rid of the problem employees. This was Larry in spades. "Irrational" was a severe understatement describing the menace that was he. Larry wasn't your, "run-of-the-mill" nut jobs. Far from it. Don knew that Larry wouldn't take the news of being jettisoned by the company very well. Not at all. It would be the perfect excuse for Larry to finally exact the revenge on his coworkers he desired so much to do. Don suddenly felt like a sitting duck to be shot at in a sick, twisted arcade game of some sort.

He sat back in his chair and looked around his office at his surroundings. An office desk, credenza and a drawing file cabinet along with his computer aided drafting station. This was his little work world in which he resided, until now, quite comfortably. He'd gotten used to his diminutive work kingdom. Somewhere, at least up until then, where he *had* felt safe. His own world. He took a drink of his coffee, thought for a moment or two, then picked up the phone and dialed. He heard it ringing and then it went to voicemail.

"Hi. You've reached Maggie Kimball in purchasing..."

At the same time, in an otherwise unoccupied women's restroom on the second floor of the same company, was enticingly attractive and ravishingly beautiful, thirty-five year old, Maggie Kimball, Don's girlfriend. She had long dark hair, beautiful brown eyes, teeth that would be the envy of any orthodontist and the cutest dimples when she smiled. She was decked out in her normal, business professional attire.

She stood before the room's mirror under a row of bright lights over the sinks and dabbed, in vain, at a coffee stain with a wet paper towel on her otherwise white blouse. *I couldn't have spilled it on my beige outfit,* she thought to herself. After a couple more attempts at defeating the stain she resigned herself with the thought, *Not much more I can do about it at the moment.* She gave up and tossed the paper towel in the trash.

This stain would become the very least of her worries in the passing days with the impending layoffs about to hit that she was unaware of and the unfortunate consequences contained therein. Blissfully unaware, she was, of the news yet to come her way and the resulting situation she was about to find herself in. Her entire world was about to be turned upside-down and set to crash. Maggie loved Don with all her heart, but her loyalty and love for him was about to be tested, to its limits—and beyond. Her patience as well.

Upstairs, on the third floor in the Executive Conference Room, a meeting of all the department heads was about to get underway. They were all seated around a long table. A large video touch-screen hung on a wall at one end of the table which was displaying only a blank screen at the moment.

John Stanton, fifty year old middle-aged middle-manager, was seated at the table amongst the other managers. With his Texan drawl, he delivered the punch line of a joke, "...and the guy said to him, 'Not with my dang dog you don't!'" Everyone laughed loudly including John, who giggle snorted at their reaction to his jest.

It was he who was the unlucky boss of the psycho employee that Don was so concerned with. He was the unfortunate one caught in a no-win situation from hell. An employee no one in their right mind would want to manage, nor supervise. One that needed to depart the company in the worst way. Time for severance and exiting.


On the second floor, Michelle Jeffries, who wore gobs of soap-opera jewelry, sat at her desk—working? No. Not working. She was lusting over an online jewelry site. Michelle was forty-five, going on twenty-five, and blonde as well. She had a shrill cackle for a laugh and "worked," if you can call it that, in a clerical position in the company's HR department. Maybe had she known about the imminent layoffs she'd be a little more—conscientious—diligent perhaps?

She scrolled through the pages until one piece in particular grabbed her attention which caused her eyes to light up and almost bulge out, cartoon like with the accompanying ahooga horn. Michelle placed the item in her online shopping cart and went to the site's checkout screen. She hastily and excitedly retrieved a credit card out of her wallet and started inputting the numbers with great anticipation.

Michelle was Maggie's best friend. There with her, through thick and thin. Maggie had no one else that she was this close to to ask for assistance. And ask she would.


Stylin' Brandon Ellis, the tall and slender, twenty-five year old Hispanic mail-room employee pushed a mail cart down the hallway on the third floor at the engineering company. He had an MP3 player in his shirt pocket and would almost always be wearing earbuds and rocking to the beat. The music from his earbuds was so loud that he sounded like the bass booming in a low-rider Chevy passing by. The movements of his youthful body stayed with the rhythm. He stopped at an open office and placed some mail in a bin.

Brandon was Don's BFF. They shared many of the same interests——including self preservation.


Forty-five year old, Japanese-American, Tommy Akino stood in front of a vending machine in a break room on the first floor of the same engineering concern trying to make up his mind about what to get. He was portly with permed black hair and glasses and was fond of wearing white long sleeve shirts with a tie, minus a jacket. He finally came to a decision on a carefully selected item, dropped some change into the machine, pressed the requisite buttons—and nothing happened. He pressed the coin return lever. Still nothing. In frustration, Akino banged on the machine with his fist. "Figures," he muttered under his breath. Akino didn't like his first name so everyone just called him "Akino."

Akino was not only in the same engineering department as Larry but was stuck having to work next door to him as well. Their offices were side-by-side. Akino would be another unwilling participant in what was to unfold in the days to come.

And then——there was, forty-five year old Larry Jenkins, who was a structural engineer at the company. He was tall and thin, with light colored curly hair, a receding hairline at the temples and wore black rimed glasses.

He sat at his desk holding a surveillance type snapshot that he had taken of Don's girlfriend, Maggie. He traced the outline of her body with his finger. As he did, he smiled like a funeral director that took your money and did your dead grandmother. His strange and irrational behavior around the office had rightfully earned him the nickname, "Scary Larry." And scary he was. On many levels and in many ways. Socially inept? Yes. Beyond. Social skills and he had never met. And if they had met, social skills would have ran away screaming as fast as it could. Larry had a very tenuous grasp on reality, and his personality, if you could even say he had one, was mercurial at best.

Even though he was in his forties, Larry remained unwed his entire life, to no surprise. Who would want that thing? He had never really had a relationship of any sort leaving him nothing but prostitutes for his entire sexually immature and sexually stunted life. Larry was adopted and had two unrelated adopted brothers, one older, one younger, each of which had been found guilty of murder, with the older having committed multiple homicides. All of this strongly argued in favor of nurture over nature. No genetic predisposition here. The odds against all three being homicidal psychopaths were astronomical. It had to be how they were raised.

But beyond that, was the easily recognizable, absolute insanity that he possessed. Larry's mental illness was cultivated. Tilled in his synapses and watered daily. They say that those who are definitively crazy have no idea that they are. He easily fell into that category and was living proof of such. Perfectly normal, he though he was. It was the rest of the world...

None of these people, not one of them, knew what was in store. It wasn't just a potential loss of a job. It was a potential loss of life———a somewhat more risky item.

The Hunter Engineering building was a sprawling, three story structure with over one thousand employees at that location in downtown Ventura. Emblazoned across the back wall of the building's large, ultra-modern lobby was the company logo in gold on a deep blue background: "HUNTER ENGINEERING."

The company's twenty year old receptionist, Jennifer, slender with long, curly auburn colored hair and black rimmed glasses sporting hot pink lipstick, was talking with a female visitor who stood at the counter. The woman signed-in on the company's register, and only a moment later, the man that she was waiting for arrived and escorted her away down one of the hallways. As they left the lobby, the reception phone rang and Jennifer picked up. "Good morning, Hunter Engineering," she said in her ebullient young voice, then she asked, "How may I direct your call?... Les Petrovitch?" She continued, "I'm sorry, he's in a meeting that may last most of the day. May I take a message?"

The meeting in the conference room was in progress. The same group of department heads were seated at the same table all listening to sixty-five year old Les Petrovitch, the company's executive vice president of operations. His silver hair went with his weathered and chiseled face. No miss-match here.

The image of a graph was on the large touch-screen. Using his finger he traced a declining line on the graph. As he did, the touch-screen's image glinted off of his eyeglasses making it difficult to even see his eyes through the glare. He summed up his presentation to the managers thusly, "Our corporate profit is in decline because of employee compensation having to increase to retain the necessary talent and expertise that we need. Our rival companies are downsizing and we are left with few options to remain competitive and solvent. The bottom line is—we must reduce our work force. We now have the unfortunate task of determining just who goes and who stays."

You could easily hear in his voice that the thought of having to terminate employees weighed heavily on him. He certainly didn't take this lightly. Quite the contrary. This was something that most employers never want to do. To some, their staff are almost like family in a way. Like letting your mother go because you're cutting back. Maybe she should have vacuumed more often. At least at this concern, they're not contemplating cutting employees in order to jack-up their executive salaries and maintain their golf club memberships plus all the perks.

Petrovitch paused, switched off the touch-screen with the remote and walked over to the head of the conference table and took his seat. The room lights came on.

"As managers," he continued, "you each know your own departments best. Last week you were asked to make recommendations for severance." He looked over at John. "John, we'll start with your department."

John cleared his throat, put on his reading glasses and opened up a file folder obviously bulging with documents. "Well, in engineerin'," he said, "we're only a little over staffed," he started off, in an obvious effort to attempt to protect his employees from the axe. All except for the one. "I have have two candidates for possible redeployment and eight for outright termination." John sat up a little. "The first of the candidates for termination," he continued, "is Larry Jenkins. He's been with the company for four years. His behavior has been problematic, borderin' on dangerous."

11

Petrovitch listened intently, having no clue what kind of employee they had been keeping around.

John continued, "Larry's been the common factor in numerous incidents with employees from the kid who delivers the mail to his fellow professionals. In one instance Larry was convinced that someone poisoned a houseplant in his office. He raged up and down the hallway screamin' accusations. The things he was sayin' were delusional. He scrawled bizarre things on a dry-erase board in the hallway near his room, all about the people who did this to him and how he was goin' to exact revenge.

"He's made numerous other threats to several employees who he's convinced are out to get him in some way, shape or form. He threatens to stalk them and, 'give them what's comin' to 'em.'"

Already concerned, Petrovitch queried, "Has there been anything else?"

John responded, "Oh, that's not the half of it." John folded his arms on the table and resumed reading aloud from the file before him. "A short time later," he continued, "he made threats to several employees that he was goin' to the company picnic and shoot everyone there."

At that point Petrovitch looked alarmed.

John looked up briefly then continued, "He was suspended for three days without pay and was supposed to attend anger management counselin' sessions—he never went."

Petrovitch slammed down the pen he was holding, hard, on the table top. Had the pen been a cat, it would now only have eight lives left. "And this guy's still around?!" Petrovitch asked sternly.

"Yup," said John, "Thanks to the company's now, two year old, rules, protocols and procedures manual, I'm not allowed to fire someone without an adequate review done by HR. I keep feedin' 'em the details of his actions, but nothin' ever comes of it. And when I ask what's takin' so long, I'm told, 'They're still reviewin' the matter.' Heck, how long does it take?"

Forty-five year old, Bob Rankin, the manager of HR looked like he wanted to be invisible or simply slide under the table and disappear.

Petrovitch angrily picked back up the pen he just jolted and jotted down a note to talk with the senior VP about correcting this apparently cumbersome new employee review protocol immediately before anything happened that they could be liable for, as well as coworker safety. After he put down the pen, with a softer landing this time, Petrovitch asked John, "I suppose there's more?"

John laughed a little nervous laugh and said, "Oh, yeah. I ain't finished yet. More recently, Larry was reprimanded for the sexual harassment of Michelle Jeffries in HR. Then, just a month ago Maggie Kimball in purchasin' filed three harassment complaints against Larry. Both women claim he made numerous unwanted advances and made repeated lewd and suggestive phone calls to them at work *and* at their homes."

Petrovitch asked, "How did he get their home numbers?"

"No clue," said John. "They never gave their numbers out. No one knows." John coughed, had a sip of water from his glass then continued, "This time the company informed Larry that he *must* begin counselin' as a condition of his continued employment. He has yet to comply."

Petrovitch was fuming at this point.

John continued to refer to Larry's file before him, "His productivity has been declinin' rapidly. Tardiness and no-shows are on the increase."

Then, completely embarrassed, John said, "And there have also been times when—uh—well..." John laughed a little, "It ain't that easy to talk about in mixed company, but, here goes... It seems that sometimes he's been masturbatin' in his office durin' workin' hours with his door closed."

All of the assembled managers were very grossed out and looked back and forth at one another in shock.

"Oh, God. No!" said Trudy Watkins, operations manager at the far end of the table.

John shrugged and said, "Sorry y'all."

Ted Sorenson, logistics manager asked, "Is this for real?"

John answered matter-of-factly, "Afraid so." A couple of the other managers then nodded knowingly about it.

Petrovitch rolled his eyes and looked totally exasperated as he shook his head and looked downward. Then, he looked back up at Rankin who was wearing an, "I'm in trouble now," look based on his facial expression and body language. Petrovitch asked Rankin, "Really??"

John continued about Larry, "Several people surroundin' his office have complained, but, nothin' gets done. I've heard it myself. There were some visitors from ExxonMobil that I was

14

escortin' to my office last week and right as we were passin' his closed door he went at it."

Petrovitch covered his face with his right hand, looked down and shook his head, "Nooooo... Not people outside of our company... In our own company is bad enough, but outsiders were exposed to this too?" he asked rhetorically. Then he looked back up and exasperatedly asked John, "So this has happened more than once?!"

"Yup," John confessed, "Sometimes now it happens almost on a daily basis."

"And you've made complaints to HR about it?" asked Petrovitch.

"I and others have, several times. Yessir. I gave up after a while. What's the point?" as John looked over at Rankin.

The manager of the records department, Josh Cameron said, "I've heard about it."

"Me, too," said Evelyn Mayfield, Hunter's IT manager.

Deroy Marten from marketing said, "I've actually heard him before. It was disgusting. I was walking by and I heard something and I thought maybe somebody was watching a porn movie or something, but as I passed by his door it sounded too clear to be on a TV. So, yeah, I can vouch for the authenticity. It's true," as he raised his eyebrows, tilted his head and shrugged a little.

Astonished that all this was going on without his knowledge, Petrovitch asked, "If all of you knew this, why didn't anyone say anything to ME about it?! I'm amazed that NO ONE told me about all of these things before?!"

"We all assumed you knew," said Cameron.

Nearly exasperated, Petrovitch said, "That's even worse that all of you thought I knew this was going on and was condoning it!"

At that point, almost as if they were cued, they ALL turned and simultaneously looked at Rankin.

Petrovitch demanded in an outraged tone, "Why didn't you let me know about this, Rankin?! Why hasn't anything been done about him?!" If Petrovitch's look could kill, Rankin would be dead about fifty times over.

Rankin attempted to evasively respond, "Well, I, er, um, because of, well, you know—Because of that."

"And what is '*that*'?" asked Petrovitch, snidely.

"Well, what I meant to say was, um..." Then, just in the nick of time, his feeble neurons had finally come up with an excuse, or actually, a scapegoat that had no idea they were being volunteered and offered up as such. Rankin continued, "I thought my staffer, Bernice had told you. I, I, I told her to." Now, she'll be one more of the candidates for termination in HR. An unwitting sacrificial substitute pawn for Rankin.

Petrovitch just stared at Rankin as Rankin avoided eye contact, lest his jig was up.

John took off his reading glasses then looked up from the file and said in summation, "I and others think he is a potential 'Time Bomb' ready to go off. The overall pattern of erratic behavior is worsenin' and has been thoroughly documented—and is ——thoroughly disgustin', too."

John closed the folder and sat back in his chair as he look-

16

ed downward at the folder before him, in a hangdog fashion.

Petrovitch asked John, "So you haven't made any headway to resolve this?!"

John answered, "No." As John looked at Petrovitch, he nodded his head in Rankin's direction, and said, "You'll have to ask Bob here why they ain't done squat about this guy." John looked back at Rankin and continued, "Y'all ain't helpin' much, that's for sure." Then John turned to Petrovitch and said, "I've been dutifully reportin' all of this to HR. I assumed they were followin' through and notifyin' you. That's what I get for as-sumin' someone else was doin' their dang job."

Rankin looked at Petrovitch and was totally speechless while Petrovitch stared a hole through him filled with daggers. After a brief moment Petrovitch said, "Maybe we need to start cleaning house in HR, first?!" as he cocked his head while he looked directly at Rankin.

"Sorry sir," Rankin managed to spit out, and lamely at that.

Petrovitch huffed then turned back to address John and said, "I agree with you one hundred percent. This is the perfect time to let this one go. Effective Thursday..."


The plush, executive assistant's office of thirty year old, Sylvia Ochoa was nicely decorated with sculptures and paint-ings. There was also a sofa and a coffee table, some large potted plants and five, scale models of their engineering projects. Sylvia had worked for Petrovitch for more than seven years and was very trustworthy with the inner workings of the company at this level. If anyone knew, "Where all the bodies were buried," it would have been her. Besides her competence, for that one reason alone, her job was very secure. So that the company's secrets were secure.

Don sat on the edge of her desk and leaned over slightly toward her as she looked up at him with a smile on her face and said, "So, does your girlfriend know you're up here flirting with me?"

"Hey, we're just talking," said Don. Then he tried to—not so subtly probe with—"Oh, by the way, someone mentioned that there's some big meeting going on today."

With that, her expression changed. Right after his utterance, the phone rang before she could say anything else about it.

"Hang on." She answered the phone, "Hello, Les Petrovitch's office... I'm sorry, Mister Petrovitch is in an important conference with all of the department managers and can't be interrupted."

Don listened with keen interest.

"I'm his executive assistant," she continued, "Could I help you with anything?" She began writing something on a note pad.

Don tried to nonchalantly see what she wrote on the pad without being *too* obvious. He thought.

"OK. I'll tell him as soon as he returns. Thank you... You, too! 'Bye." She hung up the phone and caught Don trying to read the message on her note pad. She covered it with her hand.

Don asked, "So—what's the big meeting all about?"

"Whether or not to make you Vice President of the company," she sarcastically replied.

"Fun-ny."

"It's confidential," she stated. "You know I can't say anything about it."

"OK, I'll just come right out and ask; is there anything to the rumors I've heard about layoffs?"

"I knew you didn't come up here just to see me," she said with an annoyed tone, then asked, "You only wanted to prime me for information, didn't you?"

"Who? Moi?"

Sylvia began arranging papers on her desk as Don quickly stood up. She said sneeringly, "I think I hear your mother calling you—Or, maybe it's *your girlfriend.*"

"So, does this mean you're not going to tell me anything?"

"Out!" she exclaimed as she pointed at the door. Don retreated and paused in the doorway.

"Should I be sending out resumes?"

"Adios 007," she countered.

Don exited and flinched just as a pencil narrowly missed him and bounced off the doorjamb.


Maggie sat at her desk going through a spreadsheet program on her computer, tracking the company's expenses to the Nth degree. And speaking of degrees, she came equipped with some. An MBA plus a degree in accounting as well. All this and brains too. It was one of her tasks to ride herd on unnecessary capital drains. Maggie was a procurement specialist in the company's purchasing department. Negotiating contracts on behalf of Hunter and analyzing suppliers were just some of her myriad job duties. A job that hopefully, she'll get to keep. She was couple of pay grades above Don there but that wasn't a problem in their relationship. Don felt no inferiority to her over it as some men do when their wives or girlfriends make more money than they do.

Maggie had a small radio on her desk playing soft rock music while she worked which was at a low enough volume so it didn't disturb her work neighbors in adjoining offices. She stopped her chores for a moment and had a sip of tea, then glanced at a framed photo of Don that sat prominently on her desk top. She smiled dreamily at it as though he was there in person, caressing her. Don was everything she had ever hoped for in a man. Good looking, kind, intelligent, caring, honest and sensible—or so she thought at that point in time. Another sip of tea and back to work.

The music on the radio faded out and transitioned to a traffic report which then turned into the weather. The female radio announcer said, "...and the weather for Ventura, Oxnard and Point Hueneme calls for sunny skies the rest of the week. Presently it's 75 degrees at KOXN radio. Looks like it's going to be a beautiful day out there."

Then the announcer launched seamlessly into a commercial, "And speaking of a beautiful day, why not top it off with a romantic evening of fine dining overlooking the ocean..."

This caught Maggie's attention. She closed her eyes and drifted away and smiled as the announcer continued, "...at the

Spinnaker, where they offer the best seafood and steaks. The Spinnaker is located at 1501 Spinnaker Drive in Ventura, and they're open seven days a week. You deserve a relaxing evening out."

The soft rock music returned on the radio. While her eyes were still closed, just as Maggie seemed lost in a daydream, she quietly said to herself, "Yes, I do deserve..."

Suddenly, she was startled by Larry who thrust an invoice in her face. As she opened her eyes her smile instantly drained away and was replaced by a visceral revulsion which was easy to discern from the obvious look on her face. Just another example of what inured him to her.

"Here's a bill for some software," said the lunatic to her.

"Don't you believe in knocking?" she protested. Maggie reached over and turned off the radio then looked back up at him on the other side, thankfully, of her desk.

He said, "I thought you'd appreciate it if I brought it by in person," as he leered at her with a sick smile.

"I expect you to send it through the office mail like you're supposed to."

He asked, "Why you gettin' so uptight? Aren't you glad to see me?"—Yeah, right.

"Look Larry, we've been all through this before. You're not even supposed to be in my office. Get out, NOW!" Maggie vehemently demanded as she pointed at the door.

"Ah, come on Maggie, can't we forget about those harassment complaints and start over?" he asked plaintively of her, trying to look for all the world like the nice person he was so not.

And, "start over?" There was never a "start" to start over again from to begin with. He was absolutely repugnant on so many creepy levels. Layers of ick.

Fed up, Maggie picked up the phone handset. "That's it, I've had it! I'm calling Human Resources!" she said as she nervously dialed the extension. Larry's demeanor turned on a dime and he instantly flew into a rage and angrily pressed his fingers on the phone cradle, purposely disconnecting the line. Maggie attempted to slam the receiver down on his fingers, but Larry withdrew them just in time—for him.

"You bitch!" exclaimed the real Larry, who had now shown up.

Just as Larry uttered this, Don walked into Maggie's office at what couldn't have been a more opportune time for her rescue. The damsel in distress that was tied to the railroad tracks as the "Larry Express" was bearing down on her.

Maggie's eyes looked passed Larry at Don as though the cavalry had arrived. Larry turned to follow her sight line and saw Don heading straight for him as Maggie rose up out of her chair.

Don got right in Larry's grill and stated starkly, "You'd look better outside," as Don pointed toward the door to Larry.

"I had business here," Larry insisted.

"You're business in here never existed in the first place," said Don as he poked Larry in the chest with his finger. "Get outta here," Don continued emphatically, "NOW!"

"Your girlfriend here said she wants me."

An exasperated Maggie said loudly, "You're nuts!"

Larry said to Don, "I'll bet she has a tight one."

"Shut up Larry!" replied Don trying to contain his rage. Don shoved Larry backward toward the door.

"I hate guys like you," said Larry.

Don shoved him a second time. At this point they were both at the door. Larry pointed his finger miming like a gun at Don.

"Maybe I should come back here and play 'Post Office' with my .45 semi-auto," Larry threatened.

Don shoved him hard, one last time, sending him and his perversion out into the hall and slammed the door in his face. Don then went over to Maggie who was obviously really shaken by the entire incident.

He asked, "Are you OK?" as he reached her.

"Yes—I'm OK." She looked down and away.

Don took Maggie into his arms and comforted her. They stood together silently for a moment in their embrace then kissed briefly and sat on the edge of her desk, side-by-side.

"You need to call HR and tell them that Larry was threatening us," he advised.

"I was just going to but why bother? They won't do anything..." After a few seconds she asked, "Why don't they fire that freak?"

That jogged Don's memory of what he had come to inform Maggie about in the first place. "That's what I came to tell you. I got a call from an old friend at corporate headquarters up north. He said there're going to be layoffs, and it's going to happen soon. Maybe Larry finely *will* be fired." He shrugged his shoulders, "Or we will."

23

Maggie asked, "How soon?"

"He didn't know. That's all he heard."

She then asked, "How did your friend find out?"

Don laughed a little having somewhat relaxed from his encounter with Larry. "He said he overheard a conversation in a restroom."

After some peaceful silence together, Maggie said, "All this is getting to me. I'd like to go somewhere tonight and forget about this place."

"We'll go somewhere special for dinner. How's that sound?"

She jokingly said, "Our luck Larry 'll be at the next table." She finally smiled a little as her dimples returned, then continued, "I just heard an ad about a restaurant that has a great view of the ocean."

"Sounds perfect to me," said Don.

They hugged and kissed again.

"I love you Don. I don't know what I'd do without you."

"I love you so much, darling," Don answered back. He didn't know what he would do without *her*. Maggie was his absolute dream woman in every way possible. They met there at Hunter Engineering almost two years earlier in the fall. Don was in the company's cafeteria walking around with a tray of food, not sure where he would sit. While searching, Don found Maggie seated by herself eating her lunch at one of the tables and thought she was absolutely beautiful. She was a new employee on her second day there at Hunter. She had to be new because he definitely would have noticed her if she had been there at the company for a while. He couldn't believe such a gorgeous woman would be there unaccompanied. Don walked over to her table and asked, "Excuse me, are you here alone?"

She looked up, saw him and smiled instantly. She said, "Why, yes. I am alone," hoping he was angling to join her.

Doing his best Groucho Marx impersonation, Don looked her up and down and said, "Well there must be something terribly wrong with you." He abruptly turned and started to walk away, then heard her laugh loudly and turned back around to her. "I was just kidding." He came back to her table and asked, "Can I sit here with you?"

"Yes. Please do." And that was it for Maggie. Don's handsome good looks and his sense of humor instantly won her over. It was love at first sight for them both, equally. He couldn't live without her. Don's life would have been so empty had he never found Maggie. And likewise for her without him. They complimented each other perfectly.


While Larry was still on the second floor after having been thrown out of Maggie's office, he thought he'd pay a surprise visit on Michelle and walked over to the HR department. He had the hots for her as well. And he was so far out in mental left field that he really thought she, and all women, wanted him. So divorced from reality he was, he hallucinated them saying suggestive things to him, and him taking them, one-by-one, to his psycho basement for their bondage, torture and kill. The sickest of perversions were his specialty. That was his world.

Only, perversion paled in comparison to this somebody. No one anywhere could totally imagine the scenes that went on inside his head. Fortunately.

He arrived at Michelle's open door and entered her office. She was sitting at her desk and looked up at him.

Michelle asked him, "What are you doing here?!" as she instantly felt nausea brewing inside her from his mere presence.

"I thought you'd like to see me," he replied while he leered at her, as her clothing, in his mind, was flying off her body.

"For what?!" Michelle was shaking as she looked at him. "Get out of my office immediately!" she ordered.

"Nah. I think I'll just stick around. You know you want me."

Recoiling as her skin was crawling she vehemently yelled at him, "You're disgusting! Get out of here!!"

He started to walk around the desk to her. She jumped up and grabbed a letter opener and yelled for her coworker in the next office, "Jason. Please come here! Now!!" She pointed the knife at Larry and said, "Come any closer and I'll do it! I mean it!"

A second later, forty year old, tall and muscular former Navy Seal, Jason, ran into her office like a football linebacker. He saw Larry and said, "You again?!" Jason interposed himself between Michelle and the nutcase.

Michelle begged Jason, "Will you please make him leave?" Then she turned to Larry and stated, "You are NOT supposed to have any contact with me. Leave—me—alone!!"

Jason advanced slowly on Larry who put up his hands a

little and backed up and said, "OK. OK. I don't know what your problem is," as he moved over to the doorway. "Your loss Michelle."

Michelle nearly barfed at that one.

Jason tersely said, "Don't come back here."

Larry told him, "I'll do what I want, bitch," which was absurd considering scrawny Larry pitted against a Navy Seal would be a ten millisecond fight with Larry being the one that gets pulverized. And with that, Larry left. Larry was all talk when it came to his having a physical fight with someone—but not when it came to the use of a weapon.

Michelle sat down in her chair, emotionally depleted. "Thank you, Jason. I'm so glad you were here."

"Me too. Happy to help."


Just down the hallway, around the corner from Michelle's office was Bob Rankin's office, the HR manager. He was on the phone with Petrovitch and was oblivious to the commotion going on with Michelle in his own department. Typical of him.

Petrovitch said to him, "I don't want any screw-ups with this. If this guy's as bad as he's been documented to be then we need an armed guard here before we let him go."

"I couldn't agree more."

"Good. Get on it," directed Petrovitch. "Have the guard here starting Wednesday when we open up for business," he added.

"Will do sir."

Petrovitch added, "And, no more screw-ups. Got it?!" Petrovitch hung up before Rankin could respond. Rankin was lucky to have his job after allowing Larry to have hung around for so long causing so much trouble.

Rankin quickly went through their vendor list and found the security company's number. Hawk Security. Rankin dialed the number, then stood up and stretched his back while he waited.

"Hello, Hawk security," answered their receptionist.

"Yolanda Gutierrez please."

"One moment." While Rankin was on hold he sipped some of his coffee and put it back down on his desk.

"Hello, this is Yolanda."

"Um, hi, Yolanda. Bob Rankin over here at Hunter Engineering."

"Oh, hi. What can I do for you?"

"Well, we're going to be letting a few people go here at Hunter and we're going to need a guard stationed here during working hours starting Wednesday at 8 a.m."

Gutierrez stated, "Sounds good. So, I'll be sending an *unarmed* guard?" she assumed as Hunter had always previously requested.

Just as she asked Rankin this, there was a noise outside in the hallway. Rankin turned and looked in that direction. When he did, he knocked the coffee over with the telephone cord, spilling it across his desk and paperwork. He was so distracted by the incident that he didn't hear Gutierrez correctly and assumed she said, "ARMED" guard. Rankin responded hastily,

"Um, yeah yeah," not really paying attention to what was said as he frantically tried to mop up the mess he created on his desk. Unfortunately, Rankin could never mop up the bloody mess he had just contributed to through his RANK-in-competence. "Thanks Yolanda," continued Rankin, "Sorry I gotta go."

"OK. Thanks," said Gutierrez.

Rankin hung up and continued his coffee mopping operation.

Rapidly turning into the chief office gossip, Don walked into the mail room on the first floor and found Brandon standing in front of the copier as it very noisily turned out sets of copies. Brandon had his back to the door and his earbuds in and didn't detect Don's presence, so Don slowly crept up on him and simultaneously stuck his two index fingers into either side of Brandon's ribs which made him jump. Don said, "Hi!"

After the startle wore off and he recovered, Brandon laughed a little. "I didn't even hear you come in," he said as he popped out his earbuds and shut off the MP3 player.

"How could you hear me over the copier *and* you're music."

"I'm gonna get you back bro," warned Brandon.

Don looked around and saw there was no one else there but them. "I came to tell you I got a call from an old friend who said that there are going to be layoffs here."

"No shit?!" Brandon looked like his job had flashed before his eyes, the same as they say when you die your life flashes

29

before you.

"I don't know when or who or anything else, I just thought that you might want to know," Don said.

"Yeah. Thanks man. I don't want to have to go live with my parents again. That sucked!" The copier finally finished its noisy job of copying and stapling the sets of documents. Brandon withdrew them from the collating bin and said half jokingly, "Guess I should look busy."

Don nodded his head and said, "Oh, yeah. Same here."


Maggie started thinking, *I wonder if Michelle knows anything about these layoffs. She works in HR—No. If she knew, she'd say* something *to me about it, I'm sure.* A moment later, Maggie picked up the phone and dialed Michelle's extension. It rang three rings and went to her voicemail. Maggie hung up just as Michelle entered her office.

Michelle said, "Hey..."

"Oh, hi. I was just calling you," Maggie noticed Michelle looked very harried and asked, "What's wrong?"

Michelle sat down in a chair by one of the walls and said, "I just had another experience with the token mad man here."

"He was just here harassing me. He went over and bothered you too?"

"Yes. I'm still shaking. He came around my desk at me and I had to call for Jason's help from next door! I didn't know what Larry was going to do me! Jason made the thing leave."

Maggie said, "He came by here even though he's not supposed to. Don happened to show up right in time to get rid of him. He pushed Larry out into the hallway." Then she asked, "Are you going to be OK? You looked pretty shaken."

"He really scared me." Michelle laughed a little and said, "Yeah. I'm feeling better now that I'm out of my office and away from him. I'll be OK. Thanks."

Since Maggie's door was still open she leaned toward Michelle and quietly said, "Well, maybe he won't be around here anymore to bother us," then asked, "Have you heard anything about layoffs here?"

Michelle answered quietly, "No! When?"

"Don't know. I found out about it from Don just a few minutes ago."

Michelle said, "No one's said diddly to me. Of course I'm just a flunky here. You know I'm far from, 'in charge.'"

"I know. I just wondered if you'd heard."

"No——But thanks for the warning."


Larry got back to his office and looked really hot and bothered by his "social intercourse" with Maggie and Michelle just then. He was nearly hunching uncontrollably like a dog humping someone's leg. He closed his office door and went over to his desk and sat down. Larry was hornyer than a team of sex crazed Bolivian midgets! His mouth was twitching which soon followed by his whole body as though he was having a sexualized seizure of some kind. It was the same as him receiving an over stimulus of his penis, the same out of control minor jumps that would happen if someone was flipping a taser switch on and off stimulating him with each connection of the current.

Between jolts, he opened his top desk drawer and picked up a hardcore porn magazine and opened it. He began to freakishly smile as he looked at the photos. Larry had taken some of his surveillance photos of Maggie and Michelle, and other women, cut their faces out of the photos and then pasted them onto the nude bodies of the women in the porn magazine. He roughly matched the size of their heads with the women's heads and direction that they're looking in relation to the porn image. He shoved his hand down his pants and started to masturbate. He began to moan loudly enough to be heard outside in the hallway.

A female employee walked passed outside his closed room and could hear him and said to herself, "Ewe..." She winced a sicking wince and hurried away as fast as she could without spilling her coffee—or—tossing her cookies.

Larry turned page after page with his free hand. Every page in the porn mag was the same. More hardcore images of women having sex with Maggie and Michelle's faces pasted on them.

Akino was at his desk on the phone talking with John, "Yes. I'll have those figures for you by Thursday for the turbine project... Fine... Thanks. OK. 'Bye." Akino hung up and noticed the sound from next door and made a sour face. "Gack!" he said, "Not again." He reached over to the center drawer in his desk and removed a small pill bottle. He opened it and tapped out two earplugs from it into his hand. He put in both earplugs and went back to work.

Larry was really worked up at this point. He moaned even louder and ejaculated in his hand. It wasn't that he didn't realize that others could hear him, it was that he didn't care. To him, that was *normal behavior.* After a few seconds he recovered a bit and shut the magazine. He then withdrew his hand from his pants and shook it, flinging the semen off his hand all over the carpet in his office. Larry was a wack job alright. A whackin' off at the job, wack job. Larry was the name. Perversion was his sick game...


It was late afternoon. A warm onshore breeze came through from the ocean nearby carrying with it the pleasant scent of some flowers upwind with the sun still prominent in the receding afternoon sky above. The end of the work day had finally arrived. People exited the building from all of the external doors like ants coming after an intruder of some sort, swarming almost. The intruders must have been the cars in the parking lots because that was where they were swarming to. In the building's back parking lot, the sound of car engines starting up was everywhere.

Two attractively dressed female employees in their twenties, Tina and LaRonda talked about their day as they walked to their vehicles.

"I was busy all day long," complained Tina.

LaRonda agreed. "Slave drivers," she said. "I did a last-minute report for my boss. I busted my butt, and he didn't even say thank you or kiss my ass. Sometimes I wonder why I'm even here. You know, it feels like it should be Friday but it's only Monday."

Tina replied, "I hear ya... So, what'd you do this weekend?"

"My boyfriend and I went on a camping trip to Sequoia National Park."

"Sounds nice," responded Tina, "Wish I coulda gone. I had to spend my weekend packing my stuff so I can move into my new——apartment..."

It was then that the two realized they were being tailed. Stalked. By Larry. He walked along behind them about fifty feet back, ogling them as he did so in his sick overt way, raping them in his mind. They were completely naked in his synapses, tied to a bed's posts, awaiting their fate to be dished out by him. They were grist for his psycho mill. Larry had actually tried to get a vanity license plate from the California DMV which read: BTK-1. For those unfamiliar, that translated to: Bondage Torture Kill #1. The DMV wouldn't approve it even though Larry claimed it meant: Big Tall Kite #1, which made absolutely no sense at all. No sense to the sane.

The two women's conversation ceased. They looked at each other, then Tina looked back over her shoulder a little, then back at LaRonda.

"I know," said LaRonda to her, "just ignore the weirdo. I'll see you tomorrow girl..."

"Later..."

The two women parted company, Tina walked off to the

left side of the lot and LaRonda off to the right side. Larry passed the spot where the two women separated and proceeded onward to the farthest edge of the parking lot. There, he got into a dilapidated Toyota Corolla, that looked like it belonged on skid row somewhere with a family sleeping in it, or in a scrap yard ready to go through the shredder. He started it up and made a broad, slow U-turn through the now empty parking lot, exited onto the street and headed home.

Larry drove into the narrow driveway of his house, pulled up next to the residence and parked. It was a nice looking single-story home with a Spanish tile roof in an older, middle-class neighborhood of Ventura. Eighty-five year old Albert, Larry's senile next door neighbor, sat in an old, white lawn chair near Larry's driveway watering his lawn with a sprayer. At least whatever he could hit from his chair. Albert's hair was all silver and he was of average height, other than being slightly stooped over when he stood. He was a seemingly permanent lawn fixture as he was out there constantly. He was his own garden gnome. Larry wondered if he ever went inside and didn't remember ever having seen his neighbor's yard without the neighbor in it, regardless the time of day.

Larry got out of his car.

Albert waved to Larry and reported that, "The meter man came by today."

Larry paused and looked at Albert then shut the car door. "Fascinating," Larry sarcastically replied. Larry walked away from his car toward his porch.

Albert continued, "Oh, and you got some mail too."

Under his breath Larry exclaimed, "Jesus——Fucking ——Christ!" Larry didn't respond to Albert this time as he walked up the steps to his porch and got the mail out of the box. He unlocked the front door and went in, shutting the door in the neighborhood's face.

Larry's living room was devoid of any decorations or furniture except for an easy chair that was near the center of the room and a 19 inch flat-screen portable TV on a milk crate near one wall. The light fixture in the middle of the ceiling was the only light in the room. Dusty cardboard boxes were here and there against the walls. They were decorations by default.

Larry walked into the kitchen, stood at the dining room table and sorted the mail. He dumped the junk mail in the garbage and tossed the bills on the counter. Next, he opened the refrigerator and removed its sole contents: a deli sandwich and a nearly empty one gallon bottle of milk. He poured the last of the milk into a glass, then carried his dinner, as it was, into the living room where he sat down in his chair and set his dinner on the floor. He switched on the TV with the remote, then picked up and unwrapped his sandwich.

His life was as empty as his house was of furnishings. Devoid of anyone but him or anything at all, for that matter. He was the center of his scant universe. Total narcissism. Neuroses run a muck. And even with that—rather than flamboyance, he lead an almost monk-like existence of few material items and couldn't possibly have lived a more mundane, loaner lifestyle if he had tried. Larry was about as far from normal and well adjusted as one could get. Day-by-day, he became more so. More deviant. More perturbated. More extreme. More—off-the-deepend.

The Spinnaker Restaurant's decor resembled an old sailing ship. Lots of unfinished shiplap, brass adornments and knotted ropes. The late afternoon sun rays cascaded in from a louvered window and streaked across a placard on an easel which bore the heading: "Fresh Catch of the Day & Spinnaker Specials."

Two couples with drinks in hand were siting patiently waiting on a couch while the hostess was taking the name of a group of five people.

Don opened the front door for Maggie and the two entered the restaurant's lobby.

Don said, "From the looks of the parking lot, I'd say half of Ventura's here."

They both looked at all the people seated in the bar.

Maggie asked, "Did you make reservations?"

"Yeah, I did—Good thing too."

The party of five headed off to the bar and the hostess greeted Don and Maggie.

"Hi. Welcome to The Spinnaker. Do you have reservations?"

Don quipped, "You mean about eating here?"

Maggie shook her head. "Do—onnnn..." she said with a

mock annoyed tone.

The hostess courtesy laughed.

"Yes. The name's Thorp," he said.

"OK." She checked the list, found them and crossed off his name. "A booth by the window for two," she continued. The hostess picked up two menus and a wine list. "This way please."

Maggie looped her arm around Don's arm and they followed along behind.

As they proceeded through the restaurant, the hostess turned and looked back and told them, "We also have tables outside on the deck if you'd prefer."

"No," said Don, "I don't feel like having, 'seagull surprise' for dinner."

Maggie sighed. "You're embarrassing me," she said somewhat jokingly.

Don rolled his eyes and smiled.


Dinner came and went and Don and Maggie were left with the view, their nearly empty plates and their wineglasses. Their seafood meals were excellent. The restaurant was stellar. It was the kind of place that you wanted to try everything on their menu combined with wonderful, appetizing aromas in the air. Where one could remain over their plate seemingly forever exploring the culinary delights. And the view matched the quality of their food. The two sat in a booth in the main room of the restaurant next to a large window overlooking the water. Soft music was playing in the background while a waitress with a heavy tray of food passed through on her way to another table down the line.

Our couple lingered over the last of their dinner as they gazed out the window. In the distance, two small boats were bobbing in the sea, and a bright orange sun was about to touch the ocean horizon. They looked back at each other.

"This place is wonderful," she said, dreamily. How accurate she was.

He nodded his head in agreement, took another drink of wine and then reached across the table to hold Maggie's hand. They smiled at each other for a few seconds as he softly stroked his thumb back and forth on the top of her hand, then she looked away again toward the sunset. Don looked back out the window too. They enjoyed the view in peaceful silence again for a few moments. As good as this restaurant was, it still couldn't mask the situation they were facing. Only a temporary escape from the issues potentially doming them.

Maggie said, "I finally feel better after that confrontation with that sick bastard Larry today," as she had another drink of her wine and looked at Don. He looked back at her. She continued, "You know, that creep is really beginning to scare me."

"I've been worried all along," Don added, "I think he's dangerous. I'm certain he'll snap if he's fired." Worried wasn't the half of it. Not even the quarter or sixteenth of it. Run-in after run-in with the same loony person. And no support or recognition of the seriousness by their company, or at the least, very little attention paid. No awareness of the brewing situation, which was so plainly, transparently evident to Don but opaque to most others.

Maggie said, "The company should have gotten rid of him a long time ago."

Don asked, "What did HR have to say today? The same old thing?"

"Nothing of any use, as usual. I can file another complaint. That makes me feel soooo much better."

Filing complaints that fall upon deaf ears. Piles of complaints do no good unless they're addressed. HR. Human Resources. What a lovely euphemism. Just like a garbage truck worker is elevated to a "Sanitation Engineer," no less. What a lofty profession to aspire to. How many years at a university for that degree? In reality, Human Resources was only a quaint euphemism for—the Personnel Department. And beyond that, so many people erroneously assumed or believed that a company's HR department is there to protect the employees from each other or to protect them from the company itself. No. Shhhh... The secret was that HR departments are there to protect *the company* from its employees. Many a dead man and woman have put their trust in an HR department at numerous companies to rescue them in some way, from someone, only to find out, and many times too late, that it was not the case.

There was a brief silence. Maggie softly bit her lower lip.

Don said, "I thought we came here to forget about all that." Don squeezed her hand. She smiled a little, then nodded her head in agreement with him.

"You're right," she admitted. They sat there quietly together for a few more moments, soaking in the beautiful scenery

—and each other.

Then Don said, "Hey, I know. Let's go for a walk on the beach."

This made her smile broadly. "Sure. Sounds good to me."


Don and Maggie slowly walked hand-in-hand, barefoot along the water's edge. The afterglow of the sunset was still prominent on the horizon and there was a two day old crescent moon hanging in the sky. The sound of the surf came and went as it phase shifted up and down, from the low rumble of the waves coming in to the shore, to the gradually higher pitched hiss as the water receded back into the ocean before the next wave arrived. Seagull calls were all around and a flock of pelicans flew along in a loose line, paralleling the shore about one hundred yards out. The sea breeze got stronger and stronger as twilight came upon the scene. Amazingly, there were no other people on the beach for as far as they could see in either direction.

Maggie ran a couple of steps ahead of Don and turned to face him and laughed a little as she walked backward. She teased him with a quick kiss, then turned away toward the water. Don ran after her and caught her and held her tightly.

"I want you with me all the time," he said.

Maggie softly called his name, "Don..."

"You're the woman I've waited for all my life. We're perfect together." Don kissed her neck and she moaned. After a few moments they continued their walk down the beach. Don said, "I found a house online that's for sale. It's just two blocks from the beach with an incredible view..."

"Oh yeah," she said with anticipation.

Don continued, "It would be perfect for us. We could move in—right after our honeymoon."

Maggie's smile turned upside down into a frown. She asked, "Why do we have to get married?"

He said very seriously, "I'm pregnant."

Maggie laughed, then he did, too. She said, "I thought we agreed to just go on with things the way they are for now."

"We've been living together for a year," he said, then asked, "What is it about me that you're not sure of by now?"

They stopped walking and she turned to look at him and said, "Lots of couples who lived together get married and start fighting all the time and end up miserable. You know that's happened to me once already. I'm not going through that again."

He answered, "That won't be us."

"I'm afraid getting married would change us. I'm perfectly happy now," she said firmly and resolutely.

He said, "I think things would be even better. Marriage might make us closer." After a few seconds he asked, "Are you holding out for something better?"

Maggie laughed. "No. Of course not... But I don't want to talk about it now."

They embraced.

Ever since they moved in together a little over a year earlier, Don had been after her to get married. She was the most beautiful, perfect woman he could ever have hoped to meet and was paranoid about losing her to another. So, marriage, he thought, somehow guaranteed not losing the one you so ardently admired.

Maggie, on the other hand had been in an extremely bad marriage earlier in her life before she had met Don and didn't want to go down that road again. Or at least, not yet. Everything was fine with her ex until they got married. He instantly became controlling and insanely possessive and they fought all the time. She felt that she and Don were both still young enough and there was no reason to rush. Even though a year's time wasn't exactly rushing things—But still... She'd learned her lesson from before.

"You told me you'd think about it," he said.

She leaned back in his arms and looked him in the face. "Don't spoil it. You're ruining the mood."

Suddenly, a large wave immersed them up to their knees throwing the two off balance and also temporarily rescuing her from the issue. She reached for him as he grabbed her hand, preventing her fall. He pulled her to him and they kissed as the water swirled about their ankles.

Their entwined bodies were silhouetted against the amber sky out over the ocean. Don held Maggie tightly as if he would never let her go. She pulled back and slowly unbuttoned his shirt. It caught the wind like a billowing sail. She ran her hands across his bare chest as he slipped his hands down her back to her waist as they kissed ever so passionately.


In stark contrast, Larry was alone at home, slumped in his

chair, still watching TV. The sound was muted, though he just sat there in a trance-like stare, watching the images on the screen. Next to him on the floor was a dirty glass of milk and a crumpled up sandwich paper. The show he was watching, though not really listening to, ended. He stretched and yawned then looked at his watch. This was his loner life. Not even a pet. Good thing too. Had he one, it would probably be dead, knowing him. Alone and lost in his thoughts as his only companions. No one to talk to but himself. Continual reinforcement of his neuroses. Compounded annually. A constant feedback loop confirming and verifying any paranoid suspicions.

Larry picked up the glass and the crumpled paper off the floor then went over to the TV and shut it off. He ambled into the kitchen, tossed the paper into the garbage and rinsed out the glass setting it in the sink. He passed back through the living room, switched off the light and headed down the hallway in the darkness.

Arriving at his bedroom, Larry pushed open the door. His lone figure was rimmed by a cold, greenish-blue light from the hallway. He entered the dark and still room.

Through half open blinds, well focused slits of light from a street light streaked across Larry's body as he undressed. He disappeared into the master bathroom and flicked on the light switch. A shaft of light from the bathroom flooded onto Larry's bed and the wall beside it. In the lit up part of the wall were surveillance type photos of several women pinned to it. There were some of Maggie and Michelle, plus other women mixed in—some coworkers, some strangers. Larry was a stalker on top of it all. Following, photographing and putting them into his twisted menagerie of would-be and fantasy victims for his sick pleasures, plus to use their cutout faces in his porn magazines.

Oh, if he could have ever done anything he'd ever wanted —look out. Captives in his imaginary zoo, at his perverted disposal, for whenever he felt like going on a spree as it were. Psychiatry and medications? Could those have saved him from himself? Doubtful. Reasoning and chemical compounds won't always work. Some people are on a different wavelength than the majority. A different channel no one else can get. Lucky for most of us. Larry was one of those kind of individuals. The ones you *never* want to encounter or cross paths with————You'll live longer.

The toilet flushed and the shower started.

# TUESDAY

*MARK J. WILSON*

Layoffs. The rumor had spread far and wide and already after just one day the entire building's staff had heard of what was coming their direction. The fact that roughly ten percent of those who worked there would come to know, all too well. All too personally.

Akino sat in his office using a 3D engineering application on his computer. He was deeply engrossed with his work, so much so that he didn't notice—him—show up. Then he suddenly heard, "Hey, Nip!" Akino did a double take and looked toward his doorway. There stood the menace that was Larry.

Akino was astonished at what he thought he heard and asked, "What??"

"I said, 'Hey—Nip!' Did you hear me that time?" Larry asked in a snotty tone.

Akino angrily asked, "What is it with you, anyway?!" No one wanted to have any interactions with this thing if they could help it. It would have been wonderful, Akino thought, if his office had been on the farthest side of the building from here. Even better, a building in another state, on the other side of the country from here, instead of—right next door. Akino had won the negative lottery and had done his level best to escape the majority of possible exchanges with the disturbed prick next door, but sometimes, no matter how you avoid something, IT tracks you down and *you're* in its sights. Blindfolded on a tight rope. Safety net not included.

Now that Larry had Akino's attention, Larry asked, "How're you doin' it?!"

Akino asked seriously, "Doing what?!"

"Don't fuck with me and play games," Larry said.

Akino shook his head and wondered if this was all real and then asked, "What?!" again.

Larry said menacingly, "When I was in Iraq, we learned all sorts of ways of dealing with the enemy."

"Huh??"

"I'm gonna ask you one more time. How—are you doing it?"

"OK. I give up. What in the hell is it that you think I'm doing?!"

"Making—that—high—pitched—noise!" Larry was so wound up at this point that his head was nearly sideways by the time he finished his declaratory sentence.

With a truly confused look on his face Akino emphatically answered, "I don't hear anything!"

"Right..." said Larry nodding disbelievingly.

"No. Really, I don't," implored Akino.

"That's funny. That's exactly what that mail room fuck said too. 'I don't hear anything,'" he said with a mocking, juvenile tone, then said, "That proves you're in on it with him! I know what you're up to and I'm gonna make it stop."

"What the hell are you talking about?!"

"You know damn well what I'm talking about!" Larry said.

"No, 'damn well,' I don't!" said Akino, now becoming more and more worried about his own personal safety. Then he told Larry, "Hey, man. Just leave me alone! I've had it with this crap from you!"

"Oh, yeah? What're you gonna do about it?" said Larry with, not a chip, but a whole fireplace log on his shoulder.

"I'm going to file another complaint about you with HR. And now—I'm considering getting an attorney."

Larry answered back menacingly, "You're gonna need an undertaker when I'm done with you."

Akino stood up at his desk and said, "Don't threaten me!"

Larry said, "It's no threat you Jap piece of shit. It's a promise." Larry turned and went back to his office. Halfway between his office and Akino's he yelled back, "Stop with that sound, Jape, or else!"

Akino looked like he was going to deflate after being so hyper-pumped-up. He shook his head, went over to his door, shut and locked it. He heard what sounded like Larry hitting the wall between their offices with his fist, hard. Hard enough to make all of the framed photos and Akino's degrees nearly jump off the wall.

Akino walked back to his desk and sat down. He took off his glasses, laid them on his desktop and looked up toward the ceiling, then closed his eyes and rubbed them with both palms. He took a few deep breaths and tried to relax—at least a little. At least enough to make the shaking go away. Why couldn't he make Larry go away? That's what he truly was in need of—desperately. After a few moments of quite solitude—once his blood pressure had diminished enough, and his temples weren't pounding anymore, he looked back at his computer screen and went to the HR site on the company's intranet to file another complaint about Larry. The SEVENTH one! *Why me?* he though to himself. Then he thought, *It's not just me. It's every-one here, I guess. Why the hell did John ever hire this guy?... He must've interviewed really great or something!*

John stood next to his filing cabinet with the top drawer open looking for something he had misfiled. He heard a soft knock at his door, looked up and saw Akino entering. John asked, "What's up. No. Let me guess. It starts with the letter, 'L.' Am I right?"

Akino walked over to John and said, "Good guess."

"What happened this time?"

"The guy's nuts, that's what happened!"

John said, "Grab a seat and sit down."

Akino responded, "I don't want to take up too much time. I'll make it brief—Why did you ever hire him?"

"Oh, well, it wasn't my doin'," stated John helplessly, who

then continued, "He was hired by Dan Glickmann up in Concord. Then they moved him down here four months after they hired him. Glickmann's the one that saddled me with him. It was about two months before I hired you. I had nothin' to do with it or any say, really. They notified me that they were transferrin' him to our location. Didn't take long to figure out *why* they dumped him on us. I'll never forgive Glickmann for that. Rat bastard.

"And now that he's here, my hands are tied because of these stupid new company policies. It has to be HR that does everythin', and they've done just the opposite—nothin'! I've reported it all to them, but, it ends up goin' nowhere."

Akino saw the frustration that John was experiencing over this untenable situation. He understood and said, "OK. That makes sense. I couldn't understand why you would have ever hired that maniac in the first place."

John shrugged his shoulders and said, "There ya go. I didn't, nor would I have. I knew it from the first day he walked in here—somethin' wasn't right about him. Just got worse as time went on and, now, here we are." John wanted to tell Akino that Larry was being terminated on Thursday but he didn't want it getting around to Larry somehow. The fewer who knew, the better. He said to Akino, "Don't worry. It'll all workout soon," then winked at Akino without saying anything specific and therein gave him some hope to cling to.

Akino slowly nodded an understanding nod and smiled vaguely.

It was just after lunch at the company and there was rock music coming from a boom-box in the engineering conference room. John was seated on a stool with a stupid party hat on. Behind him on the wall, a large, colorful banner read: "Happy Birthday John!" There were dozens of balloons, a birthday cake and about thirty-five employees who were celebrating. They were all down for a party anytime there was an excuse. One more reason productivity had fallen. Slacker employees. "Stay at your desk and answer your phone, the job you save, may be your own," said someone of bygone workplaces once. A time of a different work principle. How times have changed.

Off to the side, two young women in their twenties were talking, Amy and Jenna. Jenna was a recent hire.

Jenna asked Amy, "Everyone's here but Larry. Shouldn't we go get him?"

Amy asked, "What?! Are you out of your mind?! Scary Larry?" She then added, "You're new here. You don't know about this guy. You think we call him 'Scary Larry' for nothing?" Actually, "Scary" was totally inadequate. "*Terrifying* Larry" was more like it. Much more descriptive and accurate. Much closer to home.

"He doesn't look so scary to me," said Jenna naively and unawaredly, then continued, "Well, I'm going to let him know." Good luck. People don't get reputations for no reason at all. There was a reason alright.

Amy said, "OK, but I'm going with you for your own safety."

Jenna poo-pooed Amy's admonishment of the necessity of

a chaperon but accepted it just the same. The two exited the party just as everyone sang, "Happy Birthday To You." John blew out the candles on the cake and all cheered.


The two young women arrived at Larry's open door. They looked in and saw Larry just sitting at his desk as he stared blankly out the window. He didn't notice them at all. He was so still, he might have been a mannequin sitting in a diorama of a typical 21st century office scene in a museum of business offices somewhere.

Jenna looked at Amy who in return nodded her head toward Larry. Then Jenna knocked softly on the door.

Larry suddenly jumped up out of his seat as though he were launched by a giant, super coiled up spring, which in turn caused the two women jump almost out of their skins considering who they were dealing with. He then silently stared at them, making them feel very uneasy. Very—uneasy. It was all starting to sink-in for the new hire. *Now* she understood, quite clearly.

Jenna shyly asked Larry, "Uh... we just... uh, wanted to know if you're coming to John's birthday party in the engineering conference room? Everybody is there but you."

He continued his extra creepy, trance-like stare at them.

The women looked at each other and then back at him.

A smile slowly formed on his face. This was *not* a good sign. "A birthday party... For John, huh?"

Amy took over for the now speechless Jenna, and said very

curtly and abruptly to him, "Well, we'll be going now!" She tugged her friend's arm, who at this point was frozen like a deer in Larry's headlights, and they both escaped speedily from his ambience, post haste.

Larry laughed a dark laugh.

Which creeped out, even more, the two young women as they walked away from Larry's office at a brisk, scared pace. Their skins were almost crawling faster than they were moving. As they scurried away Amy turned to the newbie and said, "I told you!"

"I should've listened!" admitted Miss previously dubious and extremely naive.

After a few seconds, Larry exited his office with a crazed look on his face and headed down the hallway toward the conference room pell-mell, where the soon to be ruined festivities were taking place.


At the party, the boom-box was playing a different piece of music with Brandon acting as the DJ. Don maneuvered his way through partiers as he balanced two cups of punch and two plates of cake. He made it over to Maggie and handed her cake and punch to her.

"Thanks." She set her punch down on a table and had a bite of cake. "I can never pass up birthday cake," she admitted.

"Same here," agreed Don. "Although, one time I saw a guy inadvertently spitting all over the cake as he blew out the candles."

"Ick," reacted Maggie as she looked at her slice with a raised eyebrow.

"But, ever since that, I've always made sure I was there when the candles got blown out. The cake's OK."

The smile came back to her face and she resumed eating, once assured.

"Sorry. I hope I didn't gross you out," said Don.

"A little. Glad I know now. I never thought of that."

John and Michelle were dancing in the center of the room while the crowd hooted and hollered, egging them on.

"Looks like they're having fun," Don observed.

Amy and Jenna returned through one of the conference room entrances. A scant fifteen seconds later, Larry came through the same entrance and walked right up behind John. He slapped his left hand onto John's shoulder causing him to stop dancing. Michelle noticed and stopped as well with first a confused and then repulsed look on her face. Gesturing like his right hand was a gun, Larry stuck his finger up to the back of John's head.

The crowd was shocked and stunned into silence. Brandon cut the music which had been juxtaposing the bizarre scene that was unfolding. John appeared very concerned as he looked sideways, back at Larry who was grinning ear-to-ear.

Larry said to the crowd, "Wouldn't it be exciting to stick a gun at the back of someone's head and slowly squeeze the trigger and blow their brains all over the room?" He laughed a demented, super sicking laugh, then continued with, "What a rush!"

The crowd gasped in horror.

"You're sick Larry!"

"He's nuts!"

"He's fuckin' crazy!" exclaimed several of the no longer partiers. Turn out the lights.

"Going Postal" never felt so good! Larry laughed loudly at all of them.


Larry got back to his office and was still sickly laughing over his performance just a couple of minutes earlier at John's party. He was almost shaking, seizure-like as he laughed. A weird, vibratory, whole body, jerking laugh. He could see himself actually doing it, for real, in his visions of distortion. Visions where there was a *very fine line* between reality and "Larry's reality." Two incongruous items. A tenuous border between light and very, very dark. A dangerous gray area. Realities that are polar opposites, like the poles on a magnet, never to meet. In Larry's mind it was no different than if he really had done it. In the party in his mind, they're all there. The ones he would shoot if he ever had his way: John; Don; Maggie; Michelle; Akino; Brandon; and whoever else crossed him, or his path, for that matter. Then he thought...

John walked into Larry's office knocking him out of his fantasy trance. A slap in the face back to reality, nebulous though it was.

John was both tired of it all and now scared to be put in this position by Larry or to have any interactions with him. He said, "Larry, I'm sendin' you home for the day."

Larry looked truly astonished. "What for?"

Exasperated, John asked rhetorically, "'What for??'" then continued, "You gotta be kiddin' me?! For your little theater of the absurd where you shoot you boss in the head! That's what for!" John was visibly shaking from dealing with him.

Larry said, "That was just a birthday joke," then delusionally added, "Didn't you see how everyone laughed?"

John looked at him slack jawed at how divorced from reality he was. So divorced, there wasn't even a joint custody arrangement between him and reality.

John said, "Look, I don't know what planet that would be a joke on, but not here on this one it ain't! Anyway—go home for the day... You know Larry, you're on thin ice here with your job."

Larry was shocked, "You'd fire me over just a joke?!"

John had his little nervous laugh at the ridiculous absurdity of it, the only thing that helped him deal with all of this and said, "It's not just that Larry, and you know it."

Not playing dumb in the slightest and with utmost sincerity Larry said, "I dunno what you're talkin' about. I'm your best employee, and you know it!" Yes, he was delusional. And John was speechless. Larry *was* the best employee in that "Devil's Workshop" everyone refers to. John was at the point where he was clawing to hold onto *his own sanity* dealing with this nutball and said, "I'm not arguin' anymore. Go home. Now!"

"Fine. You're not hurtin' me none."

Larry left the room, and hopefully the office for the day.

But then there was always tomorrow and whatever that

could bring, which could be anything where Larry's concerned. John thought, *Just one more day to get through with him tomorrow and then that's it! So long!* He stood there alone for a few moments, then left Larry's office, bound for HR.

Michelle had already returned to her office after the spectacle that Larry had put everyone through that was in attendance. She was at her desk inputting data into a spreadsheet program on her computer. Yes, she was actually working for a change. So, now, she was trying to accomplish the tasks she was supposed to do contained within her job description. It's amazing what a rumor about losing your job did for productivity around the building.

John knocked on her door.

She looked up from her work and asked, "Oh, hey. Are you OK after that?"

John shook his head and said, "It takes all kinds."

"All kinds of nuts!"

"You got that right," he chuckled. "I sent him home for the day. What else can I do. My dang hands are tied by the company and their, just as insane as Larry is, rules. It'll be the death of us all."

"Oooo, don't say that," Michelle advised.

"Good point. Bad phrase to use. Anyway, is Bob in?"

"No. He's supposed to be back in an hour or so."

John said, "Oh, well. Doesn't seem to matter if he's here or not."

Nodding yes, "I know what you mean," agreed Michelle.

"There ya go," John said like a true Texan. Texan is an entirely different language. For instance, the question in English would be, "Did you eat?" In Texan it was, "Jeet?"

Then John added, "Oh, and I forgot, thanks for the birthday party, before it got rained on anyway."

Michelle attempted to sing, "Someone left the cake out in the rain..." John snickered and she broke out into her shrill cackle, both repeatedly. Music could be heard approaching. Not paying any attention to it, John turned around and bumped into Brandon as he entered the room carrying a small box. She laughed a little. "I could hear you a mile away," she said to him.

He yelled back, "What?!—Oh, yeah," he said and shut off his MP3 player.

"Much better," she said.

John said, "Hey, Brandon. While you're here, thanks for being the DJ at my party."

"Cool. Sorry about what happened," Brandon said.

"Yeah, thanks. It wasn't your fault, by any means, but, yeah, thanks. Anyway, I gotta run."

Michelle and Brandon said, "Good-bye," in unison as John headed out the door.

Brandon turned to Michelle, "Here's that package you've been waiting for," as he set it down on her desk.

"Thanks," she said, then asked quietly, "Did you hear about the possibility of layoffs here?"

"Yeah. Don warned me yesterday," he said, then continued, "I can't afford to lose my job, that's for sure."

"Unless you're lucky enough to win the lottery, who can?"

"No more slakin'," said Brandon.

Then after a few seconds, Brandon asked, "Can you believe what Larry did at John's party today? I've seen it all now. Isn't the company going to do anything about that dude?"

Michelle started cutting open the box.

"At this point," she said, "I'd believe anything about that freak. Personally, I think he should be fired—or arrested," she offered, "but all John could do was just send him home for the rest of the day."

"That's crazy," Brandon said, then laughed and added, "*He's crazy!* When I dropped off a package in his office the other day he asked me if I could hear a high-pitched noise. I told him I didn't hear anything. And get this—he said the noise was coming from Akino's office right next door, and that Akino was trying to drive him crazy. I told Larry, 'It'd be a short drive' for him, and then he got all pissed-off at me and then said that I was in on it with Akino!"

"He's paranoid to the max," said Michelle.

"Yeah, he's trippin' alright. I thought I was gonna get into a fight with him... So..." Brandon asked, "What's in the box?"

Michelle finished unwrapping a necklace made of white beads and topaz-colored glass squares set in silver. She held it up to her neck and asked in an excited manner, "What do you think? Does it go with my eyes?"

Brandon squirmed as he feigned approval. "Uh, well, gotta get goin'," he said as he bailed out of her office at twelve thousand feet.

About twenty minutes after Brandon left Michelle's office he was on his mail run up on the third floor and was outside Larry's office. He parked the mail-cart near his doorway, went through the folders and got out Larry's mail, took a deep breath and went into his office. Larry wasn't there! *Cool! not here*, Brandon thought. He placed the mail on Larry's desk, turned around and came face-to-face with Larry.

He scared the hell out of Brandon who reflexively screamed, "Agghhh!!"

Larry asked, "What the fuck are you doin' in here while I'm gone?!"

"Nothin'! I just put your mail on your desk. That's all!"

"I don't believe you. I know you were doin' somethin' in here or planting something in here! Where is it?!"

Brandon just stared at him. Anything he said to crazy man would be construed into something far flung from reasonable but he said something anyway, "Dude, I thought you were gone for the day."

Then, Larry's non sequitur, paranoid mental ant farm in his head suddenly came up with, "I'll bet you're the one that poisoned my houseplant, aren't you, you fuck!" Truth was, Larry never watered it. His lack of care was its downfall, not some paranoid delusion that someone else had a scheme to do anything with it.

Brandon shook his head emphatically and said, "I don't know what you're talkin' about man!"

63

"Liar. Tell me what you hid in here, now! And, what'd you do to my plant?!"

"I didn't do anything!"

Brandon tried to leave his office and Larry got in front of him and blocked his egress. Brandon started to go around him and Larry put his hand out to stop him.

Brandon sternly warned him, "Do not touch me!"

The two were about the same height only Brandon was more muscular and half Larry's age. If Larry wanted a fight, he didn't want it with Brandon. He would lose to Brandon and lose badly. Brandon went around him out into the hallway followed closely by Larry who kicked over Brandon's mail cart, knocking it to the floor and scattering the folders and employee mail about.

Brandon said, "You asshole!"

Larry laughed, then his facial muscles started twitching visibly. He paranoidly hated Brandon so much for whatever it was he was convinced that Brandon had tried to do, he pointed his finger at Brandon, miming a gun again and went, "Bang!" at Brandon. "You'll be dead fucker!"

Brandon just looked at him in shock.

Larry had the most insane look anyone could ever have on their face and went back into his office and slammed the door shut, shaking the wall slightly.

"Good riddance," said Brandon under his breath as he righted the cart and began picking up the scrambled mess o' mail off of the floor and resorting it there in the hallway, uncomfortably close to you-know-who.

After a few seconds, Akino cautiously came out of his office and quietly said to Brandon, "I heard some of that. Are you OK guy?"

Brandon quietly said, "Yeah," nodded his head and then added, "Now he thinks I killed some plant he had or something."

"Figures," said Akino. "You need any help?"

"Oh—uh, no. Thanks though."


It was in the late afternoon that the new, office hours security guard, thirty year old Eric Slater arrived. He was a buffed out former Marine with a blond crew cut and wore a uniform with a security company badge. He entered the front doors and approached Jennifer at the reception desk.

"Hi. I'm here to see Mr. Rankin," he said to her.

"Certainly. Your name?"

"Eric Slater, with Hawk Security."

"Thanks." She dialed that extension and waited for a few seconds, then said, "Hi. This is Jennifer. I have a Mr. Slater here from Hawk Security to see you... OK." She hung up and said to Slater, "He'll be right down. You can have a seat over there if you'd like." She pointed out the sofas and chairs on the other side of the lobby.

"Oh, no. I appreciate it. I sit around enough."

She laughed a little. "Me too. Especially with this job."

"Yeah. It's the same for me with mine. Half the time I'm on my rounds, the other half, just sittin' A—round... So, you're Jennifer and I'm, well, you already know, Eric."

She smiled and giggled a little and stuck out her hand and they shook, "Pleased to meet you," she said.

"Likewise," replied Slater, who smiled back at her. Slater then walked away toward the center of the large room and looked around at everything there. Situational awareness.

A few moments later, the lobby elevator chimed and opened and out walked Rankin. He saw Slater in his uniform and approached him. Rankin said, "You must be Slater."

"That I am. I'm the person they've assigned to your company," he responded and the two shook hands.

Rankin said, "Let's go over here to the guard station." They walked over to that part of the lobby and stopped. "This is your post. It's here for the two 'off hours' guards that work here from your company." He looked around to make sure no one was within earshot of them and quietly said, "We're having layoffs here on Thursday and thought it would be prudent to have someone from your company here during the daytime."

"OK."

"We'll want you to start here tomorrow morning at 8 a.m. We don't think we'll have any problems, but if we do, there's one person that we're the most concerned about." Rankin reached into his suit jacket pocket and withdrew his smart phone. He used his thumb to navigate to the company's mugshot photo roster and found Larry's photo and enlarged it with his thumb and index finger. He showed it to Slater. "This is the guy. Larry Jenkins."

"Got it."

Rankin didn't fill him in any further. The details about

Larry were important, but not important enough for Rankin to communicate them to the person assigned to deal with whatever occurred. And even though Slater was in his uniform for the orientation, Rankin didn't see any weapon on his duty belt but just assumed he didn't bring it that day. He thought the the guard would bring it the next day when he started. NEVER ASSUME. Yet another mistake with ramifications far beyond its original benign simplicity—and by the same inept individual. The "Peter Principal" in action. Rankin had been promoted to the level where he was no longer competent.

It was nearing evening. A row of tall palm trees separated a parking area from the two-story apartment building in Ventura where Don and Maggie lived. The building's pink stucco shone warmly with the accompanying white trim in the late afternoon sun. The last light of day enveloped the mountains in the distance while large cumulus clouds dotted the blue sky above.

The two lived on the second floor near the front, or street side of their long, straight apartment building which was about ten minutes from the ocean.

Maggie sat on the sofa in their living room with her legs tucked under her as Don entered from the kitchen and set a bowl of seedless purple grapes on their kidney-shaped coffee table. He sat down next to her. The stresses of the day slowly melted away as they watched the evening news show. But even there, they had no respite. No escape from the stresses of their workplace in particular which had followed them home like a puppy. A very lethal and insane puppy that will do more than just chew your favorite slippers. The TV reminded them of what they endeavored to forget—Larry.

On the TV was a female news anchor with a map of Nevada on the screen behind her. She was just finishing the last of an air crash story.

"A spokesman for the FAA said that pilot error was at fault for the crash. There were no survivors," said the news anchor.

Then the image cut to a female reporter in her late twenties with microphone in hand who looked like she was waiting for a cue to do a stand-up. Behind her was a yellow, "DO NOT CROSS – POLICE LINE" tape and a three story office building farther behind. The news anchor then introduced the live shot, "And now we go to Terri Marino live at the scene of that late breaking story in Pacoima, California. Terri..." as she handed it off.

Marino began, "I'm standing in front of the Epson Oil Company offices, where, at 4:15 this afternoon, a disgruntled employee that was fired two days ago returned to his former workplace and went on a shooting rampage..."

Don quickly grabbed the remote and turned up the volume.

A now louder Marino continued, "...killing seven and wounding thirteen former coworkers. Then, he turned the gun on himself." The image cut to a photo of the murderer, a white male in his forties holding a beer in his hand with five other individuals standing in a garage. The area around his face was lightened so he would stand out. He had a crazy look on his face reminiscent of Larry. Marino continued, "The police have identified the gunman as forty-five year old, Vernon Harris, who worked in this building for six years."

Just what Don and Maggie needed to hear. The threat that was Larry followed them in many forms. Stalking them without even having to do so directly. Stalking by proxy.

The image cut back to the reporter as she stepped over to a woman in her fifties and a man in his forties standing nearby. Marino said, "With me is an employee of the company, Betty Pierson. Betty, please tell us about your experience in there earlier."

Marino put the mic in front of Pierson. Pierson's eyes were red and puffy from crying and she was still jittery.

"Uh, well," Pierson began, "we were in the break room when we heard like shots and people screaming. Uh, then we saw, uh, people like running in the hallway and heard more shots. I've never been through anything like this before."

"Fortunately, few of us have," interjected Marino who then asked, "What did you do next?"

Pierson "like" stated, "We all, uh, like decided to make a run for it and get outside. We never saw him."

Marino followed up with, "Did you know Mister Harris or work with him?"

"Oh, yes," said Pierson, "For five years. Nobody here liked him very much. Uh, he was like a loner, you know, and it seemed like he was, uh, like always causing trouble for somebody here at work."

Don looked at Maggie. "That sounds exactly like Larry," he declared. Too much like Larry. Too close to home—Too late to defend against? The wheels were turning in Don's mind now. Wheels of instinctual self preservation, not to merely run defenselessly away, hoping beyond hope that there wasn't a deadly roadblock in the hallway named Larry and being left with absolutely nowhere to run.

"Thank you, Mrs. Pierson," said Marino who then moved on to the man standing there next to Pierson. "Also with me is Forensic Psychiatrist, Dr. Martin Carlson from the California Occupational Safety and Health Administration, who specializes in workplace violence. Dr. Carlson, thank you for being here on short notice."

"Certainly. That's normal for these kind of things," he said.

"Yes, I guess it is," she admitted. "With these kinds of incidents on the rise, what are some of the things that employees can do to prepare for a situation like this?"

Carlson responded, "Employees don't necessarily have to resort to meeting violence with violence."

Don looked incredulous. "Yeah, tell that to the dead ones," he pontificated. Indeed...

Carlson continued, "An employee could look for a safe hiding place, plan an escape route and plan where to meet up with friends on the outside in safety."

A plan.

That's what Don was in need of. But solely an escape plan?

Or a response plan instead? *Why react defenselessly? Why be reactive instead of proactive?* he wondered to himself. Why be a hopeless sitting duck when there could be an alternate defensive measure? Yes—defense. But how? What? How do you not fight fire with fire? Fighting firearm *with* firearm was the only credible alternative that he could come up with. Larry would love an excuse to go on a shooting rampage, Don surmised. Getting fired and exacting his revenge is more than just a remote possibility. An actuarial table of happenings and their odds of occurrence would back that up. And Larry getting fired was just what Don expected. Larry had always threatened gun usage. His threats had meat on them, not the bare bones of most who would never pursue such a horrible thing. But Larry. Larry may as well have been a character written to do as much—with a gun. For a certainty.

*How could I smuggle a gun into work for our protection,* mused Don internally. *No firearms allowed at work. And I don't even have a gun. Where would I ever get one in only a few days?* He thought further, *There are waiting periods. We could be dead by the time the waiting period ends.*

Don shook his head at the situation as Maggie munched grapes while watching the TV, oblivious to his internalized plan formation.


Larry sat in his chair in his living room watching the same interview of Dr. Carlson at the massacre.

Carlson continued, "Troubled employees should seek

counseling if they feel like they're running out of options and that they're considering violence. These are very important things to pay attention to."

Larry smirked.

"It could help keep one of these psychopathic killers from exploding at your workplace when they come back gunning for someone they know," Carlson concluded.

Larry admired the mass murderer that the news was focused on at the moment. He fantasized continually about himself doing a massacre exactly like the sicko they were talking about on the news, only ten times worse with ten times the casualties. He could see himself chasing his most hated coworkers down and into a corner and blasting away. Most would find it abhorrent, but it actually excited Larry and made him want to emulate the scenario.


Don and Maggie were still seated on the couch. Don muted the TV and turned to her. "That's just what I'm afraid Larry's going to do," he said to her.

Maggie added, "That lady could have been describing Larry. But still though, I really don't think he'd ever actually go through with something like that. Those kinds of things are rare."

"I don't know about that," Don replied as he began to attack the grapes as well after the distraction.

"I wouldn't take him so seriously. You're just being paranoid," Maggie diagnosed, then continued, "He's crazy but he's probably not *that* crazy."

Don shook his head and thought, *Is everyone blind to this but me?*

Maggie added, "Those kind of things don't happen except in the movies," she said in total denial of the elephant holding a gun in its trunk in the room that no one but Don would admit to it seemed.

"We weren't watching a movie right now," Don said to her, "It was *the news*. It was *reality*. All of those dead people thought the same thing. They probably thought it would just be another day like every other day there. I doubt any of them expected to die."

She scoffed yet again at his prescient prophecy of doom. "You're turning into a nervous Nelly. I wouldn't worry about it," she said dismissively.

Don shook his head.


Larry got up from his chair, turned down the sound on the TV and walked over to the window and peeked out of the blinds. The street was still bathed by the amber glow of sundown. He had the window open a little for some air. Only the sound of crickets, an occasional car and a TV a few doors down could be heard. Larry scanned the street and then looked next door. He saw Albert sitting in his lawn chair as he stared into nothingness, as usual. "Old idiot," Larry said. He then fantasized about cracking the window open farther and discretely dispatching the old codger with one quick, clean shot to the back of his head. So cleanly surgical, that it wouldn't even knock off his straw hat when it bisected his corpus callosum and came out of his forehead on its way across the street, somewhere downrange.

Larry turned, and with a broad, unhinged smile, walked away from the window, having just seen it all happen in his mind. So satisfying it was...

# WEDNESDAY

*MARK J. WILSON*

The Hunter Engineering building was lit by a low angle, golden morning sun which cast long shadows from the eucalyptus trees surrounding it and the structure itself. Freeway traffic noise competed in earnest with the area's birds.

On the first floor, in drafting, the door to Don's darkened office was open. Don hadn't arrived yet. But Larry was there uncharacteristically early that morning. He passed by the open door and took a quick glance into the office. After a couple of seconds, he reappeared and stood in the doorway. He looked back and forth and noticed no one was around and entered the room.

On Don's desk was a photograph of Maggie. Larry picked it up and ogled it. "Oooh, baby," he said. He placed the picture back on the desk and turned his attention to Don's drafting computer. "Let's see what shit-head's working on," he said to himself as he moved the mouse and brought up a piping diagram on the screen.

Larry briefly studied the diagram. "It's one of that Nip Akino's designs," he observed. Using the mouse, Larry quickly rerouted a couple of pipes on the schematic and then hit "Save." "This 'ill fuck up Don, big time," he said with a huge, evil grin on his face. Larry laughed a little, headed over to the doorway and looked out into the hall. As an afterthought, he returned to the desk and swiped the photo of Maggie. He tucked it in his waistband, covered it with his shirt and then disappeared into the hallway after having completed his sabotage on Don's schematic.

As Don turned the corner to head for his office he saw Larry coming toward him. They made eye contact as they continued walking toward each other.

Don asked, "What the hell are you doing around here?"

Larry briefly acted like he was lunging at Don—but then only said, "Boo!"

Don didn't flinch. They passed, eyes fixed on one another.

Don walked into his office, turned on the light, and looked around suspiciously. He noticed his drafting computer was awake and rushed over to the monitor. His eyes scanned the schematic on the screen. Don had spent most of his morning trying to convince himself that he had overblown Larry's possible future explosion. And now this. Whatever *it* was. Don knew in his gut that Larry's presence a few feet from his office just now wasn't happenstance. He clicked a few computer screen buttons and the printer started up. Line-by-line, its pen whizzed across the paper building the drawing.

Don intently watched the print being built. He then shifted his attention to the drawing file cabinet and opened it as the clatter of the printer continued in the background. Using his finger, Don skimmed over the drawing titles until he stopped on: "HIGH PRESSURE TANK PIPING DIAGRAM – LAST REVISION." The same title he was reprinting fresh from the computer. Don removed the rolled up blueprints from the file rack and shut the cabinet's doors. At the same time, the printer finished its work and cut off the 24 x 36 inch drawing, letting it fall semi rolled up into the printer's catch bin. Don retrieved it, rolled it up and grabbed the first piping schematic that he took out of the cabinet.

He walked the short distance to the drafting department's common area. The whole way wondering what, if anything had been changed. He was certain about it but still had to confirm his suspicions and not act on mistaken assumptions.

In the middle of the common room was a long, glass topped light table. Don entered the room carrying the two rolled up plans. He turned off the room lights and approached the table.

Upon reaching the light table he flipped on a switch on the side of it. A set of fluorescent lights flickered into existence inside the table. The light cast shadows of Don and the plans up onto the ceiling in the otherwise darkened room. He rolled out one set of plans, taped down the four corners, then unrolled the second print placing it on top of the first. He shifted the top one around, back and forth, to align the two images and then compared them.

He scanned the designs closely, meticulously pouring over every detail and finally saw that some of the piping didn't match up. *These aren't the changes I made*, he thought to himself. So much for trying to convince himself that he was overblowing this whole thing about Larry. Don was obviously right in the first instance. Larry was deadly. He angrily rolled up the plans, stuck them under his arm and left the room bound for Larry's office.

As he proceeded down the hallway, he thought, *How do I approach this? I'm sure he did it. Who else would? Just storm in there! Take the gloves off!* Of course, Don had no idea what to expect as a reaction because he was dealing with someone so far out of societal bounds it was scary—Scary Larry. He just knew it wouldn't be good, that was for sure. *And what about John? I have to let him know about this too*, he thought. He could try to get him fired, but what would that unleash? Larry was like "Alien." You don't dare try to kill it lest it spew caustic acid all over everywhere. Or here, fire it. *Larry should've been long gone by now,* Don thought.

Larry stood with his hands in his pockets by the window in his office looking out of it as Don stormed in and threw the blueprint drawings down on Larry's desk. Larry turned to look at him.

Don was livid! "Don't even try to deny it! I know what you did. If those plans got through unchecked someone might have gotten hurt or even killed by those high pressure lines!"

Larry smirked a smile and said, "Yeah."

Frustrated and revolted, Don leaned on his hands over Larry's desk trying to control his anger. Right in front of Don's face was his photo of Maggie. Don got even hotter and snapped up the picture and held it up to Larry's face. "This proves you were in my office!" he yelled at him.

"I'm through with it. You can have it back now," Larry said dryly.

"Stay out of my office," Don said. "I'll be so glad to see you get fired."

"The bastards can't get along without me. Besides they can't fire me. I have the most seniority here in engineering." Larry pulled his right hand out of his pocket and pointed at himself. "I have *nothing* to worry about." How right he was. It was *everybody else* that had something to worry about——Him.

The sun was directly overhead. The flags on the pole in front of the engineering building's lobby were flapping in the warm noon breeze. Some employees were sitting outside on nearby benches, eating their packed lunches. One woman in her forties, Juanita, came out of the front doors with a ten-speed wearing yellow biking attire and a helmet. She got on the bike and rode away from the building though the parking lot and out to the street.

The company's internal cafeteria was very crowded and busy with activity. It bore the same cafeteria smell that you would remember from a school's cafeteria. The same "institutional" food aromas, which was not meant in a disparaging fashion, but rather, more as a familiar, comforting sensation. Many conversations were going on at once above the din of plates and utensils. Maggie, Michelle and Akino were eating lunch together at one of the dozens of tables near the center of the room.

Don and Brandon were in the food line getting the last selections on their plates and then headed over to the checkout line with their trays. Don had a newspaper folded and held it under one of his arms.

"Oh, and, you'd never believe what I caught Larry doing this morning," he said to Brandon and then added, "Or, I guess you probably would, actually."

"What?"

"As I was just about to get to my office when I came to work, there was crazy man walking away from *my* office," Don continued, "My drafting computer was up and on one of the refinery plans. He rerouted some high pressure steam lines. That could've been disastrous!"

"No shit?!"

"Yeah. I charged into his office and confronted him and he acted like it was nothing."

"What an asshole!"

Don and Brandon finally made it to the cashier. "Here," said Don to Brandon, "I'll get yours for you today."

"Thanks Man! I only have about twenty bucks left til Friday."

Don turned and addressed the twenty-five year old female cashier, Deanna. "Hi. These two are together."

The cashier went over the items, tallying them while tapping on the register screen as she went over it all, then said, "That'll be $12.95."

"$12.95?!" Don asked in an astonished tone, then turned

to Brandon and asked calmly, in jest, "Did you get the lobster?" The cashier and Brandon laughed. Don stuck his debit card in the chip reader and punched-in his four digit pin.

She handed the receipt to him and said, "I'll have to go look at the line and see if we have lobster. Yum!" They all chuckled and Don and Brandon headed off into the sea of diners. With their trays of food in tow, the two of them looked around for Maggie and the rest.

Michelle noticed the two and waved them over.

Once there, Don greeted Maggie with a kiss, set his tray and newspaper on the table and sat next to her while Brandon plopped down in the empty chair between Michelle and Akino.

Don quipped, "Well, let's hope we're not all joining each other in the unemployment line soon. With any luck just Larry 'll be there." He picked up a fork and dug into his salad.

Brandon agreed, "Yeah! I wish they WOULD can his ass." Be careful what you wish for should have been more prominently on his mind.

Don continued, "But Larry doesn't think he'll be fired. He's convinced he's indispensable."

"That figures," added Akino, "He IS delusional."

"Well, I'm sure he is going to be canned," said Don.

Brandon asked the others, "Did Don tell you about this morning?" as he took a bite of his sandwich.

"No. What?" asked Maggie.

"Yeah," Michelle asked, "What?"

Don used his napkin and addressed all at the table, "This morning he snuck into my office and altered a high pressure piping plan on my computer."

Akino said, "No?!"

Then Don turned to Akino and said, "And it was on your part of the design for the refinery."

Akino said, "Figures. I'm glad you caught it before—well —before someone died." Akino had a really shocked look about him. He added, "I would have gotten the blame for it, since it was one of my designs. Bastard!"

Don said, "That's how dangerous this guy is. I confronted him over it after I found the place where he'd changed it and he just did that stupid smirk he does and thought it was funny!"

Brandon stirred a couple of packets of sugar into his iced tea. "What a sick jerk," he said then took a drink and continued, "Yesterday I put some mail on his desk. He wasn't in there, then he showed up as I was leaving and he accused me of planting something in his office. He went into the hallway and kicked my mail cart over!"

"What?!" said Maggie.

"Yeah! It took me fifteen minutes to resort all the mail! What an asshole!"

Akino said, "I heard it and saw the mail all over the place. Yesterday morning Larry showed up at my door and called me a 'Nip' and accused me of making some high pitched noise or something."

Michelle said to Brandon, "Oh, you were telling me about the noise yesterday."

"Yeah," said Brandon.

Then Maggie added, "And Michelle and I were both harassed by him again on Monday."

Akino asked Maggie, "What'd he do?"

"Oh, the usual. Comes on strong. Thinks he God's gift to women." Maggie shuddered.

"Same with me," added Michelle, "Jason from next door had to chase him away."

Maggie told Brandon and Akino, "Don had to throw the creep out of my office. That's when he went over to Michelle's."

"Disgusting," Akino said as he started eating one of his pizza slices.

Don said, "It was a damn good thing I came by her office when I did," then gulped some of his soft drink.

Brandon said, "I can't wait until we don't have to see his ugly face around here anymore."

Don set the drink cup back down and asked, "What makes you think we'll have seen the last of him?"

"You just said he's outta here, right?"

Don said, "Oh, yeah, he'll probably get fired, but knowing Larry, I wouldn't put it passed him to actually come back here with a gun and carry out his threats. That's what I meant by I don't think we'll have seen the last of him. That's what I'm so uneasy about."

Maggie chided Don, "You're just being paranoid," as she bit off the end of a carrot stick.

"I don't consider it paranoid to be worried about someone threatening to shoot his coworkers, especially someone like Larry," he answered then ate some more of his salad while opening a little table packet of saltine crackers.

Maggie asked Don, "How did you know it was Larry that changed the plans?"

"I crossed paths with him this morning coming from my office."

She probed further, "How can you be sure that *he* did it?"

"He was there, I knew it wasn't what I'd drawn, and who else would do something like that anyway? Plus, when I confronted him, he didn't deny it. He was proud of himself! That's sabotage! If he'd do that, he's capable of anything. And with him threatening to shoot all of us, I feel like a sitting duck here, with no protection by this company and no recourse."

Michelle said, "I heard that the company hired a security guard for the daytime. He'll be here from now on. He started this morning."

Don said, "I hope he has a gun."

"No," she said, "He's an unarmed security guard."

Don replied, "Wonderful. We'll have an armed Larry and an *unarmed* guard."

"Very funny," responded Maggie.

Don said vehemently, "I'm not trying to be funny."

Michelle said, "You know what they say, once you go postal you never go back."

They all laughed except for Don who said, "I'm glad you can find humor in this situation."

Akino said, "So, they think they've got this place covered with just one, unarmed guard. That's a joke," as he finished his soft drink.

Don held up the newspaper to show the group and said,

"Look at the headline in today's paper. It's about a workplace massacre." The headline read: "DEATH IN THE WORKPLACE – 12 MURDERED." A grisly photo accompanied the story above the fold in the center of the page. More workplace terrors from workplace terrors.

Brandon said, "Oh, I really feel safe now."

Don pointed at a pull-out quote emboldened in the text. He poked that part of the page a few times with his index finger. "See this quote from one of the survivors," he said as he cited the pull-out, "'If only I'd had my gun with me.'"

"Let me see that," said Brandon. Don handed the paper to him.

"If I had a gun," Don added, "I'd be tempted to bring it to work."

Maggie set her sandwich down and—*shot*—a look at Don. "Well, then I'm glad you don't have one," she said sternly to him with a displeased look on her face.

"I know where you can get one..." Brandon volunteered.

Maggie looked suspiciously at Brandon then at Don, then back at Brandon.

"...If you want," Brandon continued.

Maggie said, "I suppose it involves something illegal."

"Not to mention, it's probably hot, too," added Michelle.

Brandon said to Don, "Well, let's just say, it's there if you need it." Brandon went back to his sandwich.

"One person with a gun could stop him," Don theorized, "I know I'd feel a lot safer if someone other than Larry had a gun around here."

Now quite concerned, Maggie said, "Larry doesn't have a gun here," then asked, "What do you think this is, the 'Wild West?'"

Don just looked at her as he took another bite of his salad and chewed it in an annoyed manner.

Michelle sarcastically asked, "OK, who wants to be Sheriff?"

Everyone chuckled except Don.

After a brief silence Akino said, "Man, the thought of Larry coming back here with a gun scares the hell out of me." Then he asked, "You really think he's that crazy?"

"If HE isn't," said Don, "nobody else in the world would ever be. You know Larry. Doesn't that sound exactly like something he'd do?" Larry would fit right into the FBI's profile for someone that would. No denying that. As much as they had tried to talk themselves out of the reality they were facing from their workplace menace, it didn't change the facts of the matter. In too many cases, denial can be harmful or even fatal.

Maggie asked, "Has anyone talked to the police?" You mean the people that show up *after* all the shooting's over?

"They won't do anything until Larry actually tries something," answered Don.

Just then Brandon excitedly pointed toward the entrance. "Look out! It's Larry! He's got a gun!" he loudly exclaimed. Brandon covered his head with his arms, Akino dove under the table, Don threw himself in front of Maggie and Michelle ducked.

The occupants of the tables nearby observing this were

88

completely perplexed.

Then, Brandon started to laugh hysterically as they all realize they'd been had.

Don annoyedly asked, "Don't you know you're not supposed to yell 'Larry' in a crowded lunch room?"

As Brandon wiped the tears from his eyes, he accidentally dumped his glass of iced tea in own his lap which caused him to shriek loudly. They all laughed at *him* now in a group display of schadenfreude.


A few minutes after lunch, Don strode up to the receptionist's counter in the lobby. He carried a digital SLR camera, a clipboard with folded up plans and a hardhat.

"I'm off to do some photos at the refinery construction site," he informed Jennifer.

"Naked women?" she asked jokingly.

"Sure. If I see any!" They laughed over their impropriety.

"Here're the keys," she said to him, "The car's in slot number seven."

Don was an amateur, wanna-be, professional photographer and fancied himself as having the talent for it.

"Thanks." Don tried to do a quick candid shot of her handing the keys to him for the pool car. She ducked and covered her face just in time. He then said, "I'm going to sneak up on you one of these days and snap your picture."

She laughed and stuck her tongue out, mockingly.

*This time* Don was ready with the camera.

89

Click/Flash!

"Gotcha!" he exclaimed.

"I hope I broke your camera!"

Don headed for the front doors, turned around and while walking backward replied, "It's the company's camera. Not mine." He then turned back around still heading for the doors.

She laughed and hid her face with one hand while she peeked through her fingers, and waved good-bye with the other as he went out the front doors.

After about five minutes had passed, Larry showed up at the receptionist's counter. "Hey sexy baby," he said to Jennifer. She looked up, saw it was him and answered disgustedly, "Oh, it's *you*."

"You look a little uptight," he said to her, then revoltingly asked, "Why don't you let me loosen you up a bit?"

"I don't think so," she said as repelled as a Sunday School teacher would be by an adult theater.

"I need a car, hot stuff," he said as he looked at her sitting, stark naked, in her chair behind the front desk.

"What's your destination?" she asked while she tossed the keys onto the counter at the perv which slid to a stop near him. Keys to the crummiest pool car they had. Her skin was crawling because she knew he was probably raping her in his mind at that moment.

He was. He had her bent over her desk, still totally nude with him behind her. The telephone cord was wrapped tightly around her neck—as people walked passed paying no heed at all. He yanked the cord harder and harder til she blacked out.

He picked up the keys and asked, "What do you wanna know for? You wanna meet me out there?"

"NooooO. You know I have to put it on the checkout form," she replied perfunctorily.

He answered, "The new refinery."

"Really," she said, then added, "You just missed Don Thorp. He left for the same place a few minutes ago." Then she wondered, *Why the hell did I tell that to this creep?*

Larry said, "Oh, yeah?" Suddenly he had thoughts of creating some calamitous accident that he could engineer to kill Don there. He smiled a sinister smile and took off for the front doors. Once at the doors, he put his back to one of the doors and started to push it open a little and said, "Well cutie, if you change your mind, you know where to find me." He winked at her and exited the door.

As the door shut she said, "Barf."


Don reached the new refinery construction site which was about fifteen minutes south from Hunter, parked and exited his pool car with all the items he had brought with him.

The site covered nearly a square mile of dirt about a half mile from the oil tankers' marine terminal near Point Hueneme. Much of the construction had already taken place. There were several large oil storage tanks and five, two hundred foot tall distillation towers, each with its own wraparound, spiral staircase. There were multiple crews welding, cutting, fabricating and constructing various elements of the design spread out all over the property. That coupled with an army of bulldozers and other sundry earth movers and scrapers. And all of this with plenty of construction noise. There was seemingly constant noise of some sort going on at any particular moment in all sectors of the refinery-to-be.

Amidst all of this pandemonium as he walked into the site, Don was distracted by thoughts. Inescapable thoughts. *What would have happened* if I hadn't seen Larry *in the morning by my office? I would have received the blame for it just like Akino would. Those are* MY initials *in the title block on the blueprints.*

Someone gets their leg cut in half just walking by, or the entire pipe ruptures right next to a person, blowing them to bits. Those were real possibilities when you're dealing with *hundreds* of pounds per square inch of pressure squirting out of a pipe never meant to hold that pressure back. And Larry was so cavalier about it all. Others' lives meant nothing to him. Beyond that, it was bordering on a sport or even some weird sexual tie-in for him. Sex and death. Together again.

There was so much about all of this from Larry that it had become difficult for Don to concentrate on his work. But Don pushed on, focused on his tasks at hand... Larry. That evil thing was invading Don's mind. No shut off valve—Work. Focus on work. It was somewhat like worrying about things you can't do anything about, such as, death and taxes. Only thing was, death was potentially waiting right around the corner, not decades from now at Don's age. Work. Focus on work.

He finally reached the middle of the new construction site where he had to check that some piping racks were built to specs.

"As-Builts" they're called. Sometimes things have to be changed slightly or weren't done exactly as drawn in the record drawings, so As-Builts are required for future operations by the plant's personnel.

Don looked upward at some piping racks, then back at the plans in his hands, then back up at the racks. He was wearing his hardhat with the "Hunter Engineering" logo on the front and making notes on the plans with a pencil. His camera hung from the strap around his neck and he would stop and make photographs with it as he went, documenting piping runs while always looking for potential artistic photographs to make at the same time for his portfolio.

About six hundred feet away in the site's parking lot, Larry parked and got out of the pool car that he was driving. His eyes roved across the mass of twisted pipes and tanks——searching. He asked himself, "Where's that shit-head?" Larry slammed the car door and went hunting for Don. Literally, not figuratively hunting. The demented engineer in Larry was out to engineer Don's demise, if at all possible. There were so many other eyes out there it hindered Larry's amorphous plans. It would have to look like an accident. Larry out "devioused" the Devil himself. If the Devil's in the details, there was Larry.

Totally unaware that he was prey of any sort out there, Don used a measuring tape to check the distance between two pipes. He noted the distance and released the measuring tape which recoiled noisily back into its case. Don noted the measurement on the plans, then ran the tape out again between a ladder and the side of one of the smaller holding tanks and noted that measurement.

Larry walked out from behind a wall, spotted Don and quickly jumped back behind the cover of the wall.

Don heard something behind him. He turned to look, saw nothing and assumed it was some construction sound reflecting from the structures nearby. Next, he set off for a group of storage tanks that were three stories tall about thirty yards away.

Larry stalked him the whole way. Don was Larry's quarry in his sick mind. Out there poaching as it were on someone else's property. *Too bad I don't have my .45 with me,* Larry thought. *With all this noise, no one would think twice about the sound. It'd be just another loud bang—And he'd be just as dead!* Larry laughed to himself. No one working there at the site was even aware that Larry was hunting Don. Everyone else was too busy with their own bailiwicks—plus—who would have suspected?

Don stopped near the base of one of the tanks. He raised his camera up and focused on some gauges that were mounted on a small stand next to the tank.

Simultaneously, on the far side of the same structure, Larry found the access ladder to the top of the two tanks and quietly climbed up to the tank's roof. Each roof of the tanks was a huge, open expanse of flat metal with a very slight pitch radiating from the tank's center outward to the edges where there was a protective railing. Larry crept along the roof of the tank, not wanting to make a noise to spook his target below. He reached a catwalk joining the tanks and eased silently out onto it. Larry was excited beyond belief to be after *this* prey. He hated Don with a super passion. His death would be an ecstatic thrill beyond belief. He craved Don's demise like a junkie craved slamming. He was "Jonesing" for his chief rival's destruction and wanted so badly to catch up with his multiple homicides sibling now residing in San Quentin. A disgustingly perverted sibling rivalry.

High above Don, Larry stealthily moved along the catwalk while watching Don below. Don had no idea what was overhead. Attempted death. Not manslaughter. Homicide—first degree. Planned out in advance. Not the happenstance of second degree.

Don saw a composition that caught his artistic eye of a set of green painted piping that was running cross ways to another set of light blue pipes, next to the tank, that were strikingly back-lit by the afternoon sun. He made a photograph of them, then rotated the camera to vertical for a different composition of the same subjects.

Larry reached the top of the tank right above Don. He looked around and saw a large pipe wrench that someone had forgotten about, left behind, next to a hatch on the roof. It weighed about twenty pounds. The wrench's weight coupled with the kinetic energy from the acceleration of a three story fall should've done the trick. Larry was thrilled with this discovery of something that was formerly a tool, that, in Larry's hands, would have been transformed into a weapon to be used to dispatch Don once and for all. A tool of destruction.

Larry quietly walked over, picked it up and moved over to the edge of the tank right above Don——or where Don was anyway. But not now. Larry was furious that Don had somehow escaped. He looked all over the place below and didn't see him.

Then, he quietly circled the tank's circumference and found him. Don had walked about a third of the way around the eighty foot wide tank and was making another photograph. Having reacquired his game, Larry slowly crept right up to the edge and looked over the side at Don, thirty feet below. Just a deadly accident waiting to happen after someone carelessly left the wrench up there. A projectile from above. After a few seconds, Larry held the wrench out directly over Don's head, he estimated ——and let go.

At the same instant, luckily for Don, he moved a foot to the right to do another photo. The wrench missed him by only inches, striking the ground with a loud CLANG, hitting with so much force that it bounced twice, nearly reducing Don to another construction casualty statistic. Startled, Don instantly jumped backward and put his hand on top of his hardhat, looked up and saw Larry looking down at him.

Larry said, "Fuck! I missed!" to Don with a chuckle.

"You miserable sonofabitch!!"

Larry laughed. "I missed you—this time."

Don was totally exasperated! He threateningly said, "There's only one ladder off of this tank and I'm going to be waiting for you right at the bottom of it!"

Larry flipped Don the bird and walked away from the edge, out of sight. Don made his way around the circumference of the tank toward the ladder. That was it for him. He'd had plenty enough! Adrenaline was flowing hard and fast in Don's veins now. *That wrench could have killed me!* Don thought. *I'm not about to forget about it or try to rationalize it away anymore. This sick bastard* IS *trying to kill me!* This meant business now, and it was the business that he was going to dispense upon Larry.

In short order, Don reached the other side of the tank where the ladder was. He leaned against the ladder with his arms folded—waiting. This time, *Larry* was the prey. For now, anyway.

Larry knew what awaited him at the bottom of the ladder's rungs. Don. A pretty well pissed-off Don.

Don peered up the ladder's length to the end of the catwalk thirty feet above. *Several* minutes later, Larry eventually appeared at the edge of the tank and looked down the ladder at Don.

Don asked, "What's the matter Larry? Afraid to come down?"

"You don't scare me."

Don asked snidely, "Well, why don't you come down then?"

Larry started down the ladder, hand-over-hand. Don set the camera and clipboard down on the ground nearby. As Don returned to the ladder, he looked around to see if they were alone. Yes. They were. Good. No witnesses. Discretion was the better part of valor, or, whatever.

Larry reached the bottom of the ladder and before he knew what hit him, Don body slammed him into the side of the tank which temporarily knocked the wind out of Larry. As Larry recovered he pitifully tried to respond, like someone who's all talk and then starts trying to slap at fists coming their way. The sissy in the school yard brawl with real brawlers. After he tussled with Larry briefly, Don regained the upper-hand and placed Larry in a semi-choke hold and twisted one of his arms behind his back.

"I've had enough of this shit from you," Don said angrily to him, then added, "Stay away from me AND MAGGIE!"

Don released Larry giving him a hard shove in the direction of the parking lot. Larry stumbled a few feet, then regained his balance just in time to avoid a face-plant into the gravel. He turned and looked bitterly at Don. Larry rubbed his neck and was totally defeated. This time.

But look out. This didn't alleviate the situation in the slightest. It only made it worse. Hard to imagine. Orders of magnitude worse. Fate sealing worse. This solidified Larry's resolve to exact his revenge, best served cold, and Larry was readying to do just that, with hot lead.

Don said, "I hope they DO finally fire your ass."

"If they fire me—I've got a bullet with your name on it, bitch."

"Larry, the only thing you ever shoot off is your big mouth," retorted Don, hoping beyond hope that Larry IS all talk and no substance while totally ignoring what had just occurred. That he was merely a psycho paper tiger. A hollow, empty shell full of vitriol and no substance.

Larry turned and stomped off toward the parking lot. Don hadn't finished what he was doing at the construction site, but now—now there was something much more important to attend to. Greatly more pressing. Don needed to go back to work and tell John about all of this, today. Someone needed to know about this. John AND the police. *But it would be just my word against his*, thought Don. *What's the point there with the police?... Just so they'd know... But what if I do get a black market gun? Do I really want the police involved then? Especially when they probably wouldn't be able to stop it from happening anyway?*

Don picked up the camera and clipboard and headed for his car. He opted to leave the police out of it. For now at least.

When Don got to the refinery's parking lot he began to cross the lot and heard a car start and its engine revved up wildly. He looked to his left and saw that it was Larry. Don stopped in his tracks and walked backward a few steps, hesitating to cross the path of Larry's car. With a threatening smile, Larry motioned for Don to go ahead across the one hundred foot expanse to the other side of the lot where his pool car was parked. A deadly dash, it would be.

"NO WAY!" Don exclaimed loudly.

Larry waved him through again as he sickly nodded his head, yes, with a giant shit-eating-grin.

Again, Don emphatically shook his head, NO!

Suddenly, Larry floored it. The tires squealed as he passed by Don, leaving the parking lot, and Don, behind in a cloud of dust. Don stood there and glared at him as he flew out into the street, narrowly missing a car driving in the opposite lane.

Don shook his head and actually breathed a sigh of relief. Relief that the nightmare had driven away. Larry was worse than your worst nightmare—because *he was reality*, and there was no waking up from that. Only dying.

Larry wasn't a direct threat to Don any longer, at least for the moment. But then he thought, he's heading toward work— and Maggie. With that realization, that he may need to protect her, he hustled to the car, started it and took off toward work.

*This is so bizarre*, he thought to himself. *All the companies in the world and this psycho had to work where Maggie and I do.*

Firing, would be the last straw for Larry. The straw that broke the psycho's back.

Don was driving back to Hunter with even more thoughts flying through his head about the immanent peril that Maggie, and he, and others, faced there at work. *This has gone* wayyyy *too far for me. He's even worse than I thought.* Little did Don know, the day's attacks were just getting underway.

Don was on a four lane road, two lanes each way, about five miles north of the refinery, when, out of a side street on the right, came a car flying directly in front of Don. Don locked up the brakes to avoid a collision. In the other car was Larry with a maniacal smile plastered on his face like a freakish ventriloquist dummy as he looked out his driver's side window at Don, taunting him! He had been lying-in-wait down that side street until he observed Don approaching at sixty miles per hour and gunned-it. Don narrowly missed T-boning Larry as Larry's car fish-tailed into the street that Don was on, going in the same

direction, north. Before Larry recovered he ended up in the opposing lanes and forced two other cars to swerve violently to
avoid him. Don proceeded again up the street, behind Larry and
started to gain on him.

As Don got closer to Larry, following him in the fast lane,
Larry suddenly slammed on his brakes as Don came up behind
him. Don locked-up the brakes instantly, turned the wheel to the
right to pass him and let off of the brakes so his car rocketed off
to the right of Larry's.

At the same time, Larry floored it and swerved to the
right forcing Don to take further evasive action, moving even
farther to the right, onto the dirt shoulder and then into an open
field where he fish-tailed slightly until he recovered and came to
a dusty halt. The obscuring, thick dust cloud eventually blew
over, and, as it cleared, ahead of Don—came Larry, straight at
him at about fifty miles per hour! Don floored his vehicle and
quickly steered right then left, swerving out of the way just as
Larry charged right passed his left side, like a charging bull and
Don as the matador, having moved deftly and adroitly out of
harm's way. "¡Olé!"

By the time Larry braked and had turned his car around,
Don was long gone and nowhere to be seen. Larry pounded the
steering wheel. "Fucker got away!"


Don had made it back out onto the roadway. Even he
couldn't believe this was happening to him. About a quarter mile
up the road he turned right, into a strip mall and parked to

blend in. He sat there enraged, breathing heavily and still shaking slightly from all of the adrenaline coursing through his veins over what just had occurred. He could now add attempted vehicular homicide to Larry's growing litany of offenses. A deadly demolition derby, of sorts, with an unwilling opponent.

Larry hit the gas and sped off and tore out into the street again, searching for Don. He didn't find Don out there, but, what Larry did find, was a California Highway Patrol car. And he found it by nearly running into it on the road when he re-emerged from the dirt field without looking first for approaching traffic.

The female officer had to take immediate evasive action. She then slowed down to get behind Larry and instantly lit him up and hit the siren briefly.

While Don was sitting in his car in the strip mall parking lot he saw Larry approach with the CHP right on his tail. Larry pulled over and stopped next to the curb on the street. He stopped almost exactly in front of Don's parking lot viewpoint position about forty feet away. Don considered getting out and letting the CHP know what Larry had just tried to do, but again it would just be his word against Larry's. Don opted to lay low, not attract needless attention to himself and watch the proceedings conveniently right before him. A front row seat. *Maybe he'll get arrested*, he thought as a faint smile emerged. The effects of the adrenaline were finally diminishing.

The buxom blonde, no nonsense, female CHP officer got out of her vehicle, put on her hat and walked with a purpose to Larry's window and said tersely to Larry, "I'm officer Burge. What in the hell is your major malfunction dude??!!" Don could hear the irate officer even this far away. "Turn the car off and hand me the keys!" she said bluntly which Larry did. She threw the set of car keys on the roof of the car. Don saw Larry talking but couldn't hear him.

Larry said to the CHP, "I didn't mean to do that," he simpered.

"Well, what in the fuck DID you mean to do??!" The officer was *extremely* pissed-off, to put it mildly. "Get out of the car NOW," she directed in an intense tone. Larry opened the door, got out and stood up. Right away, the cop spun him around and had hand cuffs on him almost immediately. She said angrily, "You're just being detained right now." The officer fished a handcuff key out of her breast pocket and double locked the cuffs so they wouldn't over tighten. She then looked toward the oncoming traffic to make sure they were clear, grabbed Larry forcefully by the wrist, purposefully twisting it in the process to assert control, and marched him unceremoniously back the the front of her CHP unit. Larry was in obvious pain by this handling of him.

103

Don loved every minute of it. It was an exhilarating and rewarding schadenfreude express for him after all he had put up with from the Larry monster.


Once in front of the CHP unit, she shoved Larry over, face first onto the hood and kicked his feet apart, hard, to spread them. She then began searching him.

"Do you have any sharp objects on you or syringes?"

"No."

"Any weapons?"

"No."

Next, she asked, "Where's your ID?"

"In my wallet."

The officer felt his back right pocket, "This it?"

"Yes."

She removed the wallet from Larry's back pocket, opened it and withdrew his license. The officer referred to it after she keyed her clip-on shoulder mic, "Any wants or warrants on a Lawrence Edward Jenkins, date of birth," she had a little sarcastic laugh, "today's date, in '75." She then released the button on the mic and said to Larry, "Happy birthday—Asshole!"

Larry smirked.

While she waited for them to get back to her on the radio she asked, "So, is that your car?" She removed his face from her car's hood and stood him back up.

"No. It's a pool car from the company I work for."

"And you treat their cars like that?" The officer cocked

her head to one side and said, "I bet they'd like to know what the hell you're doing out here with their vehicle!"

Larry couldn't possibly have cared less.

She asked, "Where do you work at?"

"Hunter Engineering in Ventura."

She nodded her head as dispatch returned the info over the radio, "Subject is clear. No wants or warrants. Three speeding tickets in the last five years. No felonies. Over."

The CHP keyed her mic, "Copy."

The officer said to Larry, "You are sooooo lucky that my shift is over and I was heading back to the station and don't feel like booking you for reckless and negligent operation of a vehicle plus about five other offenses I can think of right off the top of my head! Don't you ever let me see you doing this kind of shit ever! I'm not doing an hour's worth of paperwork tonight over your stupid ass! Now get outta here and don't come back!" she directed as she removed Larry's cuffs and handed his license back to him.

Don saw the CHP remove the hand cuffs and thought this might be an opportune time to leave. He started the car, pulled back out of the space and went to the exit—the only exit—right next to the CHP's car and Larry. Don got out over the sidewalk and looked for oncoming traffic, then back at Larry and the officer. Larry caught sight of Don and was nearly frothing at the mouth. He yelled at Don, "You fucker!!"

The cop said, "Whoa! Whoa! Whoa, buddy! What in the

hell is it with you now?!" She looked over at Don as he puled out into the street and drove away, right passed them. She looked back at Larry and asked, "Do you know him or something?"

"Yeah. I work with that shit-head."

She thought briefly about arresting him as a public safety nuisance, but decided not to, again for the same reason. She wanted to go home at her normal time so she grabbed him by the arm. "Listen to me," she admonished, "Cool it! Understand?!"

Larry nodded his head, yes.

She sternly and directly said, "Good—Bye..."

He turned and walked back to the pool car, retrieved the keys from the car's roof and got in. Once inside he stuck the license back in his wallet and stuffed it in his pocket. He started the car, put on his signal *and* placatingly signaled with his left arm, then pulled away slowly and merged into the street.

The officer took off her hat and opened the door to get back in the cruiser. She stopped briefly and watched him going up the road and said, "Asshole."


Back at work in John's office, John sat on the front of his desk while Don and Larry were seated in chairs, side-by-side, two feet apart, facing him. Don and Larry were both all wound up.

"He's full of shit!" Larry yelled at John. "You know I'm not like that. Everything he said is a lie!"

Don pointed with his thumb at Larry. "This guy's really starting to get to me. I don't feel safe with him around anymore and I want to know what this company's going to do about it. He tried to kill me today. Twice!... Well?!"

John asked, "Well, do you consider what happened today to be harassment?"

"Harassment??!" Don looked at Larry then back to John. "Are you kidding me? No! *Life threatening!*" he said emphatically. "He tried to kill me! Seriously, as far as I'm concerned what he did at the refinery was homicidal! Plus trying to ambush me and then run me off the road with his pool car on the way back from the site is attempted vehicular homicide!"

"You could go to the police and maybe get a restrainin' order against him," said John offering a useless remedy. As useless as Martha Stewart giving pointers on how to make the perfect meringue without perjuring yourself.

Larry jumped out of his chair and pointed his finger at Don. "You believe this shit-head over me?!"

Don stood up, too, not wanting to cede the high ground to the now standing Larry. "And that's not all, John," Don continued while he faced Larry, "I caught Larry altering a high pressure piping design today and it might have killed someone in the process."

"That's bullshit!" yelled Larry.

John asked Larry, "Is that true?"

"Fuck no!"

Don said, "He did. I have the two versions of the plans to prove it."

"That doesn't prove shit!" Larry protested.

"This is pretty serious Larry," John said.

Don asked John annoyedly, "NOW you think it's serious??!"

John said, "Well I didn't mean to make it seem like the other things weren't."

Larry asked, "My own boss isn't even going to back me up?!" as he got in Don's face.

John quickly got between them. "Now hold on you two."

Larry said, "I was just playing a little joke and numb-nuts here goes berserk and starts choking me and shoving me around," then Larry asked John, "What're you gonna do about THAT?!"

Don exclaimed, "You could've killed me with that wrench you sick bastard!"

Larry poked his finger in Don's chest and said, "Maybe you oughta be worried."

Don shoved Larry back slightly but John stepped forward and separated them before things escalated further. "That's enough! Both of you!"

Don stepped back. "Sorry John."

Larry looked at John and said, "If you're through, I'm going back to my office. I have more important things to waste my time on." Larry walked over to the door and turned to glare at Don one last time.

When he did, John said, "No Larry. You're goin' home for the rest of the day. Make sure you're here bright and early tomorrow."

Larry huffed, turned and opened the door so hard it slammed into the wall and rebounded as he walked out into the hallway.

Don and John looked very relieved. Like a hurricane and a five tornadoes combined, times ten, just blew through, leaving them both exhausted and clinging to each other in a root cellar in Nebraska.

Don apologized, "I'm sorry. Larry brings out the worst in me I guess..."

"That's OK, I—I understand." John laughed his little nervous laugh, and added, "Really, I do."

"So, back to my original question," Don asked, "What are you going to do about him?"

John said, "I know he's been a big problem." That was like saying having your head cut off was the same as "going topless."

"Problem?? That's putting it mildly."

John was mum for a moment, assessing whether he should let the psycho-cat out of the bag, then quietly said, "Look Don, I really shouldn't be tellin' you this—and don't go spreadin' this around either—but, after tomorrow—we won't have to put up with him anymore."

"You mean you're firing him?"

John reiterated, "Like I said, don't go spreadin' it around. OK?" He winked at Don and patted him firmly and reassuringly on the shoulder.

A look of concern washed over Don. "I'm literally afraid to turn my back on him. I'm convinced he'd put a bullet through my head if he ever got the chance."

"I wouldn't take him so seriously," as John tried to console him, "He's made a lot of rash threats but today's the first time he's actually ever done anything—that I know of.'"

To which Don said, "He's never actually been fired before, either."

John said, "Larry might just be, 'All hat and no cows.'"

Don appeared perplexed.

John translated, "Hopefully he's all talk. But we'd better be cautious, just the same. For safety sake."



Don went by Maggie's office and looked in from the doorway. She wasn't there. While he was standing there he called her cell phone with his and heard hers ring on her desk. He hung up and went to his his office to ruminate on the day's events and their profound ramifications for himself and for her, the woman he adored. He couldn't bare the thought of losing her. Especially in such a horrible fashion. The only answer he kept coming back to was self defense. And the only defense against someone's firearm—is another firearm.

*Maggie would never approve of my getting a gun, especially a hot one,* he thought. *And how would I even go about it? The only way I can do this,* he theorized, *is to take Brandon up on his offer to get one in a hurry.* He never dreamed he would be in such a position. Something he hadn't sought out nor asked for. Who in their right mind would?

*And what if Maggie finds out? That'll be it for our relationship. She'll never trust me again. She'd probably leave me.* He shook his head in frustration and looked up at the ceiling. *I have to choose between losing the woman I can't live without, or losing my life—that—I can't live without.* What a horrible quandary he found himself in. *Do I give up the one I love so dearly or do I give up my life and maybe hers?* Is it better to have loved and lost than to have never loved at all, or, is it better to have lived and not lost your life than never to have lived at all?? In this case, apparently a gun was in order. A weapon in the offing. Potentially the only thing standing between Larry and Don hanging around in a casket for all eternity and perhaps Maggie, as well. The only thing that would answer hot lead, in kind. *I've gotta go track down Brandon,* he resolved, very reluctantly, once and for all.

Don traveled the short distance from the drafting department, entered the company's mail room and walked over to a female employee in her forties, Janet, who was operating one of their copiers. The copier was making so much noise that she didn't hear him approach.

"Hi," he said, scaring her.

"Oooo!" she exclaimed.

Don apologized, "I'm sorry. I guess you didn't hear me."

She recovered quickly and said, "That's OK. I've had worse."

He enquired of her, "Have you seen Brandon?"

"Oh, he should be up on the second floor on his mail run."

"Thanks," he said. "I'll make more noise next time I sneak up on you," he added jokingly and went out the door in search of his soon-to-be co-conspirator friend.

Brandon may have held the key to their survival. The only key, it seemed. A quickly procured, down and dirty (in more ways than one), potential resolution to the crisis. But since Brandon wasn't there and he'd missed him, maybe this was providence stepping-in to stop things that Don still hadn't set in motion yet. He stopped dead in the hallway assessing his problem anew. Still time to back out. No. It's a risk that's too extreme to be ignored or left to chance. The chance that the police would arrive before the body bags and the homicide squad would be needed. He had to do it, like it or not. He'd kinda gotten used to being alive. So—he continued onward, looking for Brandon.

Don trotted up the open stairway and reached the second floor and passed office after office in his quest for safety. He rounded a corner and spotted Brandon's mail cart two doors down. Don reached the cart just as Brandon emerged from the office that it was parked next to. He saw Don, smiled and pulled out his earbuds and turned down the volume.

Don said, "Ah—Just the man I was looking for."

Brandon tossed some letters into an "outgoing" bin in the bottom of the mail cart and asked, "What's up Holmes?"

"We need to talk."

Brandon paranoiacally asked, "What'd I do now?"

Don prompted, "Remember what we were talking about at lunch today?"

Brandon thought briefly then started to ask, "You mean about getting a..."

Don quickly interrupted, putting his finger to his lips... "Shhhh, shh, shh..." Don said slyly, "Uh-huh."

Brandon quietly said, "There's an empty office right up here," as he escorted him to it. Brandon pulled a set of keys out of his pocket, found the master and unlocked the door. He opened it and the two entered the darkened room, shutting the door behind them. They stood there in the dark as they conspired on their dark plan.

Don asked in a hushed tone, "Were you serious about being able to get me a gun?"

"Yeah. If you got the cash?"

"You can't tell anyone else about this. I was just talking to John and he said that they *are* firing Larry, and it's going to be tomorrow. I know he'll make good on his threats. He tried to kill me today at the refinery site with a wrench and even when I was driving back to work by running me off the road!"

"He did?! Shit!" Brandon thought for a second, then his eyes opened wide as he looked at Don in a horrible realization, "We're dead meat tomorrow man."

Don said, "For Larry, It'd be like shooting fish in a barrel and WE'RE the fish!" He continued, "The security guard doesn't even have a weapon. Somebody's got to stop him. It could be our only chance. By the time the police get here it would be recovery, not rescue."

Brandon said, "I'll call my cousin. We oughta be able to score a gun tonight."

Don added, "I need a large revolver," he said naively as though he was going shopping at some gun store with an abundant choice of weaponry.

Brandon stated, "I don't know what kind I can get on

short notice, but I'll set it up."

"You can't tell anyone about our getting a gun."

"No shit, Sherlock. I wouldn't—You either."

Don said, "Agreed—Look, Maggie's supposed to go to the movies about seven-thirty tonight with Michelle."

Brandon thought briefly and said, "Then I'll pick you up at your apartment just before eight. Bring lots of money."

Don asked, "How much?"

"At least two or three hundred."

Don was dismayed at the amount. "That much?"

"You wanna gun tonight, don't you?"


Maggie stopped by Don's office but he wasn't there. She was very concerned earlier when Don was talking about getting a gun at lunch with Brandon. This *really* bothered her. She had always been opposed to people being armed. She felt it was way too dangerous to have untrained gun handlers about. Because of that, she had to find out if he really was serious about it. That would be something that she just couldn't live with. Maggie hung around his office for a couple of minutes but he didn't return. She gave up and went out into the hallway just as Don's boss, Louis Veley, a tall, fifty year old African-American man came around the corner.

Maggie smiled and said, "Hi, Louis."

"Hey, you lookin' for Don?"

"Yeah."

Louis said, "I just saw him in the atrium."

"Oh, thanks. Glad I ran into you." Maggie turned and headed down the hallway.

The engineering building had a large atrium in the center of the structure complete with several trees and shrubs. There was a path that lead to a small footbridge which crossed over a creek. The creek flowed a little farther then cascaded into a reflection pool ringed by several benches. The cascading water cooled the area a few degrees from the world outside of their building. Since their building was three stories tall, most of the light entering the space was indirect skylight, which gave everything a soft appearance.

Don sat on one of the benches and looked very deep in concerned thought. He heard something and looked up and saw Maggie.

"Hi beautiful," he said without his usual smile attached.

"Hi." She sat next to him and asked, "Are you OK?"

He paused not knowing where to begin, then said very seriously, "Larry tried to kill me today at the refinery construction site."

Maggie looked aghast and asked worriedly, "He did? What happened?!"

"He tried to drop a giant pipe wrench from about three stories up, right on my head. It almost hit me. And then he ran me off the road coming back."

Nearly in tears, she hugged him tightly and said, "I'm so glad you're OK!"

Don wondered, *Can I successfully keep my plan from Maggie?* Then he said, "That's why I told you, trouble's coming to look for you and me and it found us. That's why I'm so worried. This guy's not bluffing. He means it! After today I'm certain. I'm telling you, he's going to come back here with a gun and kill us!"

She said, "You're probably overblowing this."

Don was beyond frustrated and nearly apoplectic with that response considering what he just told her that Larry had done. What a stretch that was. Denial can be benign or it can be lethal. With this particular individual, it fell on the latter.

Maggie asked, "Did you call the police about it?"

"No," he said, "I have nothing to prove it. It'd be his word against mine. I confronted him in John's office and he denied it all! You can't always avoid trouble. Sometimes it just comes looking for you. We don't live in a perfect world... We have to be prepared," *Oops*, he thought. Through the compulsion to confess he unwittingly outed his underlying intentions. Hoisted by his own petard as it were.

Maggie developed a suspicious look reflecting the anxiety she had over Don's consideration of arming himself and said, "Your attitude about guns and violence really bothers me."

Concerned by what she said and that she might already be onto his clandestine plot—thanks to him—he tried to play dumb and asked her with mock innocence, "My attitude about guns and violence?"

She responded, "At lunch you and Brandon were pretty cavalier about it all."

116

Don responded, "John told me he IS getting axed tomorrow. That's all the motivation he needs. He'll do it I'm tellin' you!"

Maggie pulled away and looked at Don. "It sounds to me like you might be serious about getting a gun."

"Oh, No. No, I'm—I'm not." This fairly transparent answer of his only served to fuel her doubts. His faux appeasement went over like an intuition filled lead balloon. Convincing? Nope...

She attempted to persuade him with, "You know what I think about guns and the people who use them," she said with a frown on her face as she did her best to assert her reasoning and dissuade him from this perceived folly.

"Don't worry. It's not going to happen," he said dismissively.

There was an awkward silence. Much more awkward for Don, though.

Then she said, "What I came to tell you was that management just sent out an email memo to everyone that we're all supposed to be in our offices tomorrow morning after 9 a.m. All of the supervisors are supposed to let everyone know then."

"Looks like it's coming down at the same time for everyone. That was quick," said Don. "At least we'll know if we still have a job by noon tomorrow." *But will we still be alive by noon tomorrow?* he wondered.

As they embraced he looked extremely worried.

So did she...

Don sat in his office. How could he get any work done while he was seated in his "cell" here on death row knowing that the clock's a tickin'. Death by a firing squad of one. No last meal. No clergy reciting prayers to him as they walked to the pole where Don was to be tied. And what about that call from the Governor with a last minute reprieve? The wall phone wasn't ringing. "Would you prefer a shroud or a blindfold?" Don *was* walking through the the "Valley of Death" and he *did fear evil...*

Don just sat there in his office and stared blankly at his AutoCAD computer screen, paralyzed in thought. *Can Brandon deliver instantly like this?* he wondered. Then he thought, *What if he can't line up a gun for me? What then?* He started looking around his room for potential weapons to employ. There weren't many to choose from. A pair of eighteen inch long drafting scissors? A letter opener? Against a gun? Yeah... As he looked at his very few defensive options, he then wondered, *What do flack jackets cost? And just how quickly could I get one—or two. One for Maggie? Yeah, like she's going to wear one. She still doesn't think he's serious after all this... Will she ever?*

It was then that Don realized that he should clue-in the new guard in case no one had informed *him* about the mad man that will be unleashed upon the workforce there tomorrow. And that the mad man *will be armed* unlike the guard. Bad odds. Just like Don's and Maggie's odds for survival throughout the next few days were.

A short time later that afternoon, Don entered the lobby

118

from the main hallway and looked around the room.

Jennifer noticed and asked, "Missing something?"

"Oh, hey, Jen." Don walked over to her reception counter and asked, "Where's the guard that's supposed to be out here?"

"He's on his rounds," she responded. "He should be back any time." Then she looked out the back set of lobby doors and said, "Here he comes now."

And in walked Slater through the doors.

"Thanks," Don said to Jennifer and then walked over to Slater and introduced himself. "Hi. My name's Don Thorp," as he reached out to shake Slater's hand who reciprocated.

"Eric Slater. Pleased to meet you. What can I do for you?"

Don looked around, "I'd like to have a word with you." Don nodded toward the guard station, "Can we step over there for a minute?" He lead Slater away from the receptionist's area to the opposite corner of the lobby where the guard station was located.

Once there, Don continued quietly, "Look, I don't want to sound paranoid or anything, but, has anyone from the company alerted you about someone that works here by the name of Larry Jenkins?"

"Yeah. They told me they're having layoffs tomorrow and he might be a problem. They showed me his picture and said he's the one they're most concerned with." Welcome to Under-statementland.

Don queried, "Did they tell you if he gets fired, he might come back here armed with a gun?"

Now Slater was really alarmed, though he tried to be cool

about it and not appear to be concerned, "No one said anything about a gun."

Don said, "I thought you might like to know."

"Yeah——Thanks."


At the same time, Michelle was just returning to her office and found Maggie leaning against the desk. Michelle greeted Maggie, "Hey."

Sounding very depressed in her response, Maggie said, "Hey," back.

Sensing something was amiss, Michelle asked, "OK. What's wrong?"

Maggie didn't speak right away. She wasn't sure what to say. Eventually she said, "It's Don," then fell silent once again for a moment.

"Okayyy..." said Michelle, hoping to prod her into continuing.

Maggie looked up at her and quietly confided, "I have a gut feeling that he's serious about getting a gun and bringing it to work."

"You're kidding? You mean with Brandon?"

Maggie continued, "I asked Don if he was planning on doing that. He said, 'No,' but I'm not so sure."

"He'll be fired on the spot if he gets caught with a gun here," said Michelle, "Good jobs are scarce."

Maggie said, "He has so much to lose. He's risking everything... When you and I leave for the movies tonight, let's park around the corner and watch for awhile."

Michelle looked excited, "Oh boy! Clandestine activities, I love it." Then thinking better of her inconsiderate response added, "Sorry..."

Maggie wasn't "into it" with quite the same enthusiasm that Michelle possessed, but she needed to know for sure—one way or the other.


Don and Maggie's trip home Wednesday afternoon after work was a quiet one which was highly unusual for them. They had always spoken freely about a myriad of subjects, but now, stilted silence reigned supreme. Both were equally afraid to say anything, lest they jeopardize their intentions. Don had his sub-terfuge with Brandon and likewise for Maggie with Michelle. Maggie had her doubts and her women's intuition antennas up like Uncle Martin. Minute after minute of silence passed by, then Don asked, "What are we going to have for dinner?"

Maggie said, "Left overs, I guess——Why?" As though there was a deeper, more sinister meaning to his question per-haps.

"—Just—asking. That's all." He felt that she was highly suspicious of him. He had better be extremely careful not to tip her off, at least any further, even though it appeared that it didn't matter what he said, she would now be distrustful of it. Pick it apart, bit by bit. What did he really mean by that? Hmm...

They reached their apartment building, parked and got

out. Still silence. The same continued, and oppressive silence that roared. The two talked with each other all the time, but those interactions had seemed to have dried up, at least for the present. Another clue to Don that he's being watched closely, like a stake-out across from a jewelry store waiting for a rumored heist—Busted!

Once inside, Maggie went into the bedroom and changed out of her business professional attire and put on some regular street casual. She and Michelle *were* going to the movies together tonight, without Don. Maggie thought, *I should ask Don to come with us tonight and see if he does, or what excuse he comes up with*, as she came out of the hallway into the living room. Then she thought, *Not right now. I'll ask him at the last minute, that'll put more pressure on him.* A plan to reel in a 175 pound fibber. Deep sea fishing for the truth.

Don sat on the sofa. He was sorting through dozens of 8x10 inch color and B&W photos of various subjects from still lifes and portraits to abstracts and scenics. He was planning on entering a photo contest that a local photography store was sponsoring—if he lived that long. Maybe Don's last photo would be of Larry standing in his office doorway shooting at him. It would be very dramatic looking with the fire coming out of the gun barrel coupled with the crazy look on Larry's face.

Maggie walked into the kitchen and got out some dry cat food at the same time as their cat, Fiester, a large fluffy tortie male walked into the kitchen from wherever it was that he was hiding when they got home. She bent over and put some of the food in his bowl while he purred away for her. "There you are," she said to him as she petted his back, "I love you Fiester."

Maggie said to Don, "It's after six already. I'm going to warm dinner up so I'm not late."

"Sounds good." then Don asked, "What was it that we're having for leftovers?" An innocent enough question it seemed to him at the time.

Maggie asked in an annoyed tone, "You don't even remember what I made last night?"

"I'mmm—sorry..."

Then Maggie felt badly for being so terse with him. Plus, she really didn't want to let on that she was suspicious in any way so as not to spook him if he had some nefarious plan. "It's OK," she said back to him, "I'm sorry. I shouldn't have reacted that way to you." After a few seconds she offered, "It's all this stress from work I guess," as she tried to cover. She opened the fridge and removed their soon to be warmed up re-dinner. "Dinner's the pan seared chicken we had last night."

"Oh, yeah. That was good. Same veggies with it?" he asked.

"Yeah."

She placed the container of chicken in the microwave, set it and pressed start.

They weren't married yet, but because of the situation they were in, they were now suddenly on edge, like other married couples that have major disagreements, that, until now, they never had. It was just what she had been so apprehensive about happening in the first place. This was the first real test of their love and trust for one another.

Their land-line began to ring on the bar. While she was waiting for the microwave Maggie walked over and picked up, "Hello."

It was Brandon, "Oh, uh, hi Maggie. Is Don there?"

Maggie said, "Hang on," to Brandon and then told Don, "It's for you."

Don asked, "Who is it?"

"It's Brandon..."

Don did his level best to look totally cool and nonchalant about the call. He stood up and went over to the bar where Maggie handed the phone to him. "Thanks," he said to her as the microwave beeped for attention. "Hi, What's up?" Don asked with undertones of, "Oh, shit!"

Brandon said, "I set it up."

Don said, "Oh, uh, yeah, great... Sounds good to me."

From Don's awkward, wooden and non sequitur riddled response, Brandon had figured out that he may have blown Don's cover and quickly said, "Well, I'll see you later. 'Bye."

"Yeah. 'Bye." Don hung up.

Maggie asked, "What was that all about?"

As he thought fast, though not fast enough, nor persuasive enough, "Oh, he, uh, just wanted to know if I wanted to go to a basketball game with him on Saturday." Then he embellished further, "He said he won some tickets."

Maggie asked dubiously, "I thought you didn't like basketball?"

Don winged an answer, "I, er, I was, I just thought that, you know, maybe I should broaden my horizons a bit." *What an*

124

*idiotic answer*, he thought to himself. *Why did I say that?! What the hell else could I say?*

After Don's tortured response to a relatively simple to answer question, Maggie was convinced even further that something fishy was afoot.

"Your call only lasted a few seconds. He sure told you a lot, really fast..."

"Oh, uh, no. He had told me about it earlier today."

"Why did he call to tell you again?" she asked.

Don sensing his inquisition said, "He was just asking if I wanted to go now," he said defensively by accident, then corrected his attitude on the fly with, "He told me the details before, but didn't ask me to go yet." And worse it got for Don. Deeper the hole was dug.

"Oh..." she responded flatly, unconvinced with a raised eyebrow.


Brandon sat in front of his coffee table in his apartment a couple of miles away from Don and Maggie's. *I guess I really didn't need to call him, did I? Oops*, he thought to himself as he chewed off a hunk of his fast food hamburger and slurped a soft drink with it. "Looks like I'm, 'Captain Obvious'... Sorry, bro." It was fine for Brandon, he wasn't the one being tied to the rack presently and stretched until he confessed.

Slurppppp... at the bottom of the drink.

Outside of Don and Maggie's apartment building the last of the sun's amber rays were hitting the tops of the palm trees out in front. The aromas of several different dishes from several different dinners wafted through the neighborhood's air. Don and Maggie had finished their dinner and it was fast approaching 7:45 p.m.—Michelle was now over due, much to Don's dismay.

Inside their bedroom, Maggie stood in front of the mirror and finished putting on her lipstick. She puckered her lips, tilted her head a little and liked what she saw. The thing she didn't like what she saw lately, was the way Don was reacting to this whole layoff thing and Larry. *The thing where someone gets fired and they go on a shooting rampage hardly ever happens. Larry's not serious,* she told herself. Tried to convince herself, more like it. It was hard to ignore with all of Larry's history. *Those kind of things only happen in movies and on the news... Right?* she attempted to persuade herself. Reason with herself. But the news does happen, *somewhere,* doesn't it? *Don was probably just over stating what actually happened with Larry today.* Blown out of proportion, she theorized. Fed by his paranoia revolving around Larry. That's all. Nothing more.

And now all of this sneaky, hinky behavior with Don... maybe. She still couldn't be sure. Not until she saw if he went anywhere tonight without her knowing. Or, at least him thinking that she didn't know about his potential undercover excursion. This kind of cloak-and-dagger stuff wasn't something she ever wanted in her life. Who would? She was extending the benefit of the doubt to him. A trusting lifeline that hopefully wouldn't fray nor break.

Don stood next to the coffee table in their living room. He looked at the clock on the wall then walked over and anxiously looked out the window. Maggie entered the room and saw him at the window and asked, "Is Michelle here yet?"

Trying to act nonchalant, Don said, "Oh, uh, no. She should have been here fifteen minutes ago." He then went back over to the coffee table and the photographic prints and picked up two of them. "Look," he said, "I've narrowed it down to these two." He then asked, "Which one of these do you think will win the photo contest?" He held up the two photos side-by-side and showed them to her.

The first photo was a still life in color of a wine glass with an apple, an orange and a peach ringing it with a single stalk of celery stuck in the empty wineglass hanging out the top of it. It was against a dark background with a single strong light on the objects on a purposely wrinkled up table cloth.

The second was a color time exposure of a night scene of Morro Bay from the Rock looking back at the town with three power plant stacks lit up and all the various colored city lights shimmering in the water of the bay.

Maggie pointed to a third photo lying on the table, "That one." The one she chose, was a stark black and white of an extremely sun bleached dead oak tree against an almost black sky out in a field by itself with some scrub brush in front of it.

Don dropped the first two photos on the table and picked up the one Maggie indicated. "Oh...," Don raised his eyebrows and studied it, "Hmm..."

Then, there was a knock at the door. Don looked at the door then at Maggie, "I'll get it." Don set down the photo and hurried to the door, opened it a crack and peeked out.

Michelle announced, "It's me."

"It's Michelle," he said very relieved as he involuntarily subtly laughed and opened the door all the way.

"Sorry I'm late," Michelle said as she entered their living room. Maggie was further convinced by Don's suspicious behavior. Really, really suspicious. He *was* up to something and wasn't all that good at playing it off or disguising it.

Maggie said to Michelle, "Let's hurry before the movie starts." Just what Don was hoping for, that they wouldn't hang around long enough to cross paths with Brandon.

Don held open the front door for them. On her way out, Maggie kissed him. "Sure you don't want to go with us?" she probed further in order to observe his reaction.

He responded, "Nah. This is girls' night out. You two go ahead." It was all adding up in Maggie's intuition account.

Maggie smiled a faux smile and acted cool, "Ah, 'Girls' night out,' huh?"

Michelle added, "Yeah, don't wait up."

The girls laughed as they walked away.

Don waved good-bye, then shut the door and looked at his watch. He grabbed his keys off the bar, pocketed them and walked into their bedroom. He went to the closet and got out a gray canvas bag, about one foot square and a couple of inches thick that had two short straps on it. The perfect size to hide a handgun inside of. Then he went back to the living room and over to the window and looked through a slit in the blinds.

From their apartment's second story view looking down at the parking lot, he saw the two get into Michelle's hot-pink Suzuki Samurai.

All during this, Larry was parked behind a dumpster, up the street from Don and Maggie's apartment building, stalking them. He observed the apartments through a camera with a large telephoto lens that he had resting on the top of the steering wheel. Through his camera's lens he saw Michelle back out of the parking space she was in, pull out onto the street and drive toward the next intersection.

Michelle and Maggie reached the stoplight at the intersection half a block away and waited for the green left-turn arrow. As they waited, they gradually heard the loud Boom! Boom! Boom! of an approaching car stereo.

"Sounds like Brandon," said Michelle.

Just as she said that, they watched as Brandon drove right passed them in his Honda Civic. He was completely oblivious to their presence. Maggie turned to look out the rear window and saw him pull into her apartment's parking area. "I knew it!" she exclaimed. They got the green arrow light and started to turn.

"I'll make a U-turn," said Michelle.

"Park by those bushes at the corner," Maggie directed. Michelle flipped the U-turn and parked at Maggie's location of choice and left the motor running. The two could clearly see the apartments from their vantage point.

Larry had put the camera down and started his car and was about to follow them until they made their U-turn and parked. So he just sat there and watched them not knowing what they were up to.

Maggie and Michelle were still parked and waiting down the street. After a couple of minutes went by, Brandon's car reappeared in the driveway, and, just as Maggie had expected, Don was in the passenger seat!

Maggie turned to Michelle, "Follow them."

Michelle asked, "In this car? You can see us a mile away," she said incredulously of her, standing out like-a-sore-thumb, hot-pink Suzuki.

"We'll just have to stay back far enough to not be spotted," suggested Maggie.

"OK. I'll do my best," said Michelle.

Brandon pulled out and headed up the street away from the girls as the two embarked on their elicit weapons odyssey.

Michelle took off and bolted to catch up. The boys turned left at the next intersection as did Michelle, behind them.

Larry quickly made an illegal U-turn from the curb and followed the Suzuki. He was so focused on Maggie and Michelle up the street that he didn't see the boys go right passed him. He had absolutely no idea that the two were actually following Don and Brandon.

Don looked out the passenger window as Brandon drove and asked, "What in the hell did you call me for? We already had it set up."

Brandon said, "I just called to let you know it was a 'Go.'"

Don looked over at Brandon and said annoyedly, "Wonderful. Now she's even more suspicious of me because of it."

"Sorry. I thought you'd want to know."

"Now *she* probably knows, too," with an extra sarcastic, "Thanks!" Don went back to staring out the window.

Brandon asked, "You got the bread man?"

"Yeah. I hope two hundred's enough."

Brandon asked sarcastically, "Why don't you just write 'em a check?"

Don looked back at Brandon and asked, "They'll take a check?"

Brandon shook his head and rolled his eyes, "Sure, 'Captain Naive,'" he said to Don, then asked, "Are you out of your mind?"

"Sorry. I don't go out and buy a gun off the street everyday." Yes—And it showed.

Brandon advised, "These brothers want cold, hard cash."

131

Don really had no idea what he was about to get mixed up in with Brandon. But, had he known, would it have changed things?

The girls stealthily followed a short distance behind the boys and still remained undetected by them.

Maggie lamented, "I just can't believe Don is doing this after I told him how I feel about it." Now she was glad she had held out all this time and NOT gotten married after all. *What a mistake* that *would have been,* she mused. Certainly not now that she saw how deceptive he was with her. *That's what I get,* she thought to herself as they traveled down the road, tailing them.

"I wonder where they're going," posited Michelle.

"To some sleazy part of town, I'm sure..." Maggie was starting to look really upset. And rightfully so.

Larry continued to pace his car behind the girls who were totally unaware that they themselves were being tailed.

Don couldn't sit still and was even making Brandon nervous who said, "Hey, it's cool man, it's cool. It's no big deal—Chillax—Uh, let's have some music." Brandon switched on the MP3 player producing a sudden ear-splitting torrent of rap music.

Don nearly jumped out of his seat and quickly put his

hands over his ears and shouted, "Turn that shit down!!"

Brandon turned it WAY down. "Sorry man. Sorry..."


The loose "convoy" was approaching a signaled four way intersection out in the boondocks on the outskirts south of town. Brandon's car sailed through. Right after they cleared the intersection, the signals for the street the procession was on turned amber.

Michelle yelled, "Hang on!" She floored it to make the light and not lose the boys.

Maggie thought, *This is it! We're gonna die!* She held on tight to the dashboard, eyes bulging. Michelle's 4WD flew through the intersection, hitting the far side of it and bounced a couple of times into the air a little as the lights turned red.

Immediately behind them, Larry was forced to squeal to a halt at the same intersection leaving his tire smoke to float passed his car once he'd stopped.

Larry pounded the dashboard with his fist. "I'm going to lose those fucking bitches!" Larry looked around. After the last of the cross traffic cleared the intersection and he saw that there were no cops in the area, Larry ran the red light and sped off to catch up with them. He cranked his Corolla up to about 100 miles per hour. They weren't getting away from him! He grinned like he'd just won the lottery.


Maggie was very relieved that they made it through the

intersection. And, amazed she was at Michelle's driving abilities.

With disdain, Maggie said, "Looks like they're heading toward Oxnard."

"That sounds about right," Michelle added.

Oxnard had a reputation. Just like a "Bad Girl." Oxnard was one of the smaller cities that was adjacent to Ventura. The low rent version of Ventura, so-to-speak, where, evidently, illegal gun deals were more readily made. Many larger cities have these kinds of symbiotic satellite attachments nearby and are the butt of many local jokes: "What did the teenager from Oxnard say during her first sexual experience? Get off me dad, you're crushin' my cigarette," or, "What do girls from Oxnard and the 'Unabomber' have in common? They were both fingered by their brothers." And, "What part of an ox IS the nard?"

Maggie and Michelle had reached the start of the bridge across the Santa Clara River which was the boundary between Ventura to the north and Oxnard on the south, or, "The wrong side of the tracks"—or—river, in this instance. Instead of intently watching Don and Brandon up ahead, Maggie just looked out the passenger window at the river below and the amber afterglow of sunset in the sky above. She tried so hard to convince herself that this was all a bad dream that she would, at some point, awake from. It was only two nights earlier, she thought, when the sky looked the same as it did now. When they strolled the beach together in what had been euphoric bliss. What a difference two days can make in one's life. Maggie's seemingly secure world, wasn't so. It *was* secure, until it instantly shattered, fracturing into a thousand fragile pieces, each one,

134

each facet, reflecting a different part Maggie's face in a scrambled, stained glass mosaic.

Larry was rapidly closing on Michelle's 4WD. He slowed down a little once he caught sight of them a few cars up ahead. He quickly passed some of the intervening cars at the beginning of the bridge and when he was satisfied he was close enough, he slowed down to normal speed.

*They're going to Oxnard?* he thought to himself. *What the hell's in Oxnard that they'd want?* Tons of possibilities went through his mind, none of which was the correct reason. Who would have ever guessed *what* their real purpose was? Larry wasn't even close.

Brandon and Don cruised down the road. Don was staring nervously out the passenger window. "These people we're going to meet up with," he asked, "how do you know them?"

"I don't know these dudes. My cousin hangs out with 'em."

"I thought they were friends of yours," said Don.

"No no no. They're gangbangers."

Totally alarmed, Don turned and looked at Brandon, "Gangbangers?!"

"Well, you said you wanted a gun didn't you?"

Don rolled his eyes and looked back out the window as though he wanted to jump out of it at that point. *This is getting worse by the minute*, he bemoaned internally.

Brandon downplayed Don's concerns and tried to reassure him with, "Don't worry, my cousin wouldn't rip us off. We're supposed to meet him at a bar and he'll take us to meet the dudes."

*His cousin wouldn't rip us off. Well, what about the cousin's friends, the GANGBANGERS??!* thought Don. He looked over at his friend, Brandon, whom he trusted, but not some street hoodlums he knew nothing about. Nothing except that they're criminals. But, where else would you buy a gun in short order? A kid's lemonade stand? Don looked back out the window, then downward. He couldn't believe what he had gotten himself into. And this was only the beginning.

With the sun's rays now gone, it was getting darker outside as rapidly as Don's situation seemed to be. Don wondered, *Is it too late to tell him to turn around? We haven't gotten there yet. We can always turn around and go home. It's never too late.* We'll, at some point—it IS too late. He started to say something, reconsidered his situation and still choose to go full *bore* ahead with the original plan, hoping all would be well. He was just procuring a hot gun—from—gangbangers! Yeah. That's all. Yeah—What could possibly go wrong?

In Oxnard, the inner-city bar where they were supposed to meet Brandon's cousin, Beto, was old and run-down with the interior even worse than its exterior. The smell of rotten wine, piss and puke permeated the air in the dark, dingy business.

Four male establishment patrons were sitting at the bar, all of them in their fifties it appeared and all with a scruffy, unsavory look about them. The owners of the bar obviously didn't care about the state's smoking in businesses ordinances, as there was a smoldering, partially smoked cigarette laying unattended in an ashtray nearby. Its smoke drifted up to a layer in the room and hung there about four feet above the floor.

Don, clutching the canvas bag in one of his hands, entered the bar with Brandon disturbing the smoke layer in the process. All conversation ceased and everyone turned to eyeball them. The sound of dry-heave retching came from the place's rest room up a hall at the back of the room.

Don and Brandon approached the four seated at the bar. Brandon enquired of the patrons, "Is Beto around?"

One of whom turned and yelled down the hallway with a gravely voice, "Hey, Beto, someone's here to see you." Evidently, this was their paging system. Low cost and efficient.

The toilet flushed.

The bar patron turned back to Brandon and said, "He'll be right out."

Don kept asking himself, *What the hell have I gotten myself into? This is insane. I wouldn't be here if Larry wasn't insane.*

So who was more insane? Good question. The time to back out on this deal had unfortunately come and gone. Expired like a parking meter. Expired like rotting, dead meat. The kind of dead meat Don and Brandon could wind-up as. Would it be here, in this God forsaken hellhole, or at work—at the hands of

Larry?

A door down the hallway opened with a loud, nails-on-chalkboard squeak and twenty-five year old Beto, wearing shades, staggered out. He bounced off of the hallway's wall, grazing it a little and then managed to make it over to Don and Brandon. He wore gang-like attire, had slicked back, black hair with a cigarette tucked behind his left ear. Beto rubbed his stomach a little and said, "I feel lots better now," then belched extra loudly. Beto then noticed who it was that had come to see him. "Hey, blood, you made it." Beto stuck out his hand. Don observed as Brandon and Beto did a gang-style handshake, something Don would have no chance of replicating.

Brandon said to Beto, "This here's my homie," as he aimed his thumb at Don.

Beto offered to shake Don's hand.

"Hi," said Don, dripping with dread.

"Hey homie," returned Beto. Don attempted the handshake but bungled it laughably.

"Don't worry about it Homie," consoled Beto, "Let's go upstairs."

This environment was all so foreign to Don. This place. The situation. All of it. Don was white bread made out of white bread. He had never gotten anywhere close to as shady a scheme in as shady a place as this. Buying a stolen gun. He wondered how it was that he found himself there, of all places?


In the twilight outside the establishment, just down the

block, the girls were parked on the street and the motor was off. Michelle's dainty, pink Suzuki looked *very* out of place surrounded by the graffitied, urban squalor outside the bar. Litter, filth, decay, and a stained with who knows what, sidewalk was next to them. The very air surrounding them was thick with grime. The few people that they observed in the area from their 4WD looked as though they'd still be dirty after taking two showers AND a bath. But there was one good thing. They could clearly see the bar from their stakeout position with no obstructions.

Maggie looked over at Michelle and said, "We have a good vantage point here. We can see anyone coming or going."

"I wonder if the people with the gun are already there?" supposed Michelle.

"This place looks like gang heaven," observed Maggie. "I hope he's not in there for a long time. I don't feel safe here at all."

"Me either," said Michelle.

The local police probably didn't even feel safe where the girls were sitting. Maggie and Michelle were far outside of their element. They were in way over their heads and way beyond their areas of knowledge and experience. The two looked as out of place as Shirley Temple would be in a snuff film. "On the good ship Lolli—ARRGGGGG!!"

Maggie had pangs of guilt over it all. "I kind of feel badly now about telling Don that you and I were going to a movie tonight."

"We *were* going to the movies until HE changed our plans

139

for us," corrected Michelle.

"That's true," admitted Maggie. She wasn't the one sneaking around and lying about her intentions. It was HE who got HER into this mess by having to tail him here to this seedy, seamy, sleazy, squalid, decadent district of depravity.

It's a beautiful day to take a toke in this neighborhood,

A beautiful day for smoking crack,

Would you benign?

Where they were was Mr. Codger's Neighborhood. Emphasis on *Hood.*


And—half a block back from them, parked at the curb on the same side of the street, sat Larry in his car. The neon lights of the bar's blinking sign reflected in the front element of his camera's long lens.

His view through the lens showed Michelle's Suzuki and the bar beyond. Larry wondered, *What the fuck are they doin' just sittin' there? And in this place? A drug deal?... They don't do drugs...*


Maggie and Michelle waited uncomfortably in the Suzuki.

"I'm not going to just sit here anymore," declared Maggie, "I'm going in there."

Michelle answered emphatically, "Oh, no you're not!"

"Well, I hate just sitting here," Maggie said.

"We'll just have to wait," Michelle advised, "You can't go

in that place alone and I'M sure as hell not going in there with you. No way!" Good thinking finally on someone's part there at least.



In the dark, dingy hallway above the dark, dingy bar below, Beto, followed a few feet back by Don and Brandon, reached the top of some old, ten foot wide, creaky wooden stairs with a more gradual slope to them than most sets of stairs have.

Brandon turned to Don and asked him quietly, "Are you going to freak if they're smokin' crack in there?"

"No." Don answered, "I'll be cool about it." Or at least, he thought he would be.

The three entered a long darkly painted hallway. A single bare bulb that dangled from a two foot long wire which hung from the twelve foot tall ceiling was the only light. The sound of different TV's, on different shows echoed through the hallway as well as various conversations and someone yelling at their wife who started screaming. There was a thin haze of cigarette smoke across everything. Don tried his best to tune it all out and to focus on their mission there. Don's environment at that moment couldn't possibly have been more alien to him. It was as alien as the surface of Mars would have been, with or without the Martians. These individuals may as well have been Martians.



Maggie thought for a moment then developed a mischievous smile, reached into her purse and withdrew her cell

141

phone.

Michelle asked, "Are you going to do what I think you're going to do?"

"Uh-huh—I'm gonna call him."

"This 'ill be good."

Maggie hit Don's number and said, "Shhhh..." as she put it on speaker so Michelle could listen in.

Beto, still a little ahead of them, arrived at a door to one of the rooms on the right side of the hallway, stopped there and waited for Don and Brandon to catch up. Just as they arrived at the door, Don's cell started playing Roy Orbison's, "Pretty Woman." Don had a severe, "Oh, shit!" look on his face and just as Beto was about to knock on the door, Don both quietly and desperately said, "Hang on a minute," as he waved him off.

Brandon asked, "Are you gonna answer that??"

"I'd better so she doesn't think anything's up." Then he added "Shhhh..." to Brandon and Beto. Don swiped the phone to answer. "Oh, uh, hi, hon. Aren't you at the movie theater?"

"Yeah," Maggie said, "I just came out to the lobby to get some popcorn and I thought I'd call and tell you—I love you."

Michelle just shook her head.

Waves of guilt pangs washed over him, crashing on the rocks of his conscience. "I love you, too, darling," he replied.

Just then, the door of another apartment opened and two

young kids ran out into the hallway and went running and screaming right passed Don and continued down the hall.

Maggie asked, "What's that noise?" as she looked over at Michelle.

Don thought quickly and said, "Oh, I'm, I'm outside on the walkway and somebody's kids just ran by."

"That's funny," she said, turning the screws even further, "It sounds echoey—like—you're inside somewhere."

"Oh," he said, "Huh? That's weird—Must be the phone."

Maggie said, "Well, I'll let you go. I'm next in line here at the concession stand. 'Bye..."

"'Bye, hon." Don eagerly hung up and breathed a temporary sigh of relief.

As Maggie hung up she said to Michelle, "One lie after another..."

Then Don said to Beto, "OK," as he nodded his head to him in the affirmative, "We're ready now." Beto knocked on the door while Don and Brandon stood behind him.

From inside the room was the response, "Who the fuck's there?"

"It's Beto, man."

After a few seconds, a couple of locks unlatched and the door to the rented room opened. Beto entered the dimly lit apartment's living room with Don and Brandon right behind him. Brandon shut the door. The room was fairly narrow with a ten foot ceiling and a large window that faced—another building's brick wall ten feet away, so there was a stupendous view.

There were five gangbangers, all wearing the same basic attire as though it was a uniform: white T-shirts and baggy pants with tennis shoes devoid of laces. Three were sitting and two of them were standing. And, as Brandon had surmised they would be doing, through no great prescience on his part, they were indeed passing around a crack pipe. One of them, thirty year old Raymond, took a hit off of the crack pipe and after a few seconds, blew out the smoke. He stood up and approached them.

"Hey, Beto," greeted Raymond.

"Hey, Ese. This here's my cousin and his Homie. They're the ones that want a gun."

Raymond offered the pipe to Don and Brandon who both were adamant, yet diplomatic and semi-hip in their turning down of the offering. Raymond handed the pipe back to the one that handed it to him. Raymond was dressed differently from his cohorts, perhaps denoting a rank of some sort. He wore a frayed flannel shirt and knee length pants with white socks and tennis shoes, again with no laces in them. A lit cigarette dangled from his mouth and his cheek had a teardrop tattooed on it right below his left eye indicating he had murdered someone.

Without warning, Raymond pulled out a switchblade, pressed the button so it sprung open and held it right in front of Don's face. Don's eyes crossed and bulged out as he looked at it, and he thought, *This is it! I'm dead.* He thought briefly about trying to defend himself in some way but quickly thought better of it. Maybe this is OK and he would just screw things up worse. Just let this play out he thought. Maybe it's some type of initiation.

Referring to the switchblade, Raymond said, "This can kill you dead Homie," he advised, then continued, "A blade is quick." He put the knife down and leaned in toward Don and in a low voice added, "But most of all, it's quiet... What do you need a gun for Homie?" Raymond folded back the knife and pocketed it.

Don attempted to quickly recover and collect himself enough to not sound like Don Knotts. "Uhhh, for protection," he said in a nearly neutered voice.

"Is someone after you?"

"A crazy guy at work threatened to shoot me and my girlfriend."

Raymond thought briefly. You could see the little gangster hamsters in the little gangster hamster wheel in his head had begun their sojourn which lead Raymond to come up with: "You work at the Post Office?"

In the midst of this alien circumstance he found himself in, this struck Don as funny. "No," he laughed a little involuntarily, "No, man. Not at the Post Office. I work for an engineering company. If it matters at all."

"No. Don't matter. If you're some dude's target you're a

target. Makes no difference." Raymond took a drag off his cigarette then said, "If he's got a gun," stated Raymond as he blew out the smoke, "then you gotta have an equalizer, man. Got to." Raymond reached under his shirt and pulled out a chrome .44-Magnum revolver. "This .44's it." Raymond brandished the gun. "I seen a guy go down fast when he took a .44 slug. Nothin' left of his face, man. You know what happens when you get hit by a .44, man? Splat! That's what happens, man——Here. Check it out. It's a good piece." He handed the gun to Don.

Don, without thinking asked, "What's this been used for?"

Raymond looked over at his comrades. He and they slyly laughed a little knowing laugh, then Raymond looked back at Don and said, "You don't wanna know, man."

Don thought, *I sure as HELL can't get caught with this thing! Worse by the minute. I can't say "no" to this deal now. This could all go south in here quick. I'm committed now... Maybe* I should be committed *after all this.* Don looked at Brandon then back at the hand cannon. He opened the cylinder and rotated it and saw that it was empty. He then closed it, cocked the hammer, pointed it toward the ceiling and pulled the trigger——Click. Don felt a little more confident finally, smiled subtly and nodded his head to Raymond. The deal was done. "It's just what I'm looking for——How much do you want?"

"Two hundred. And I got bullets for it, too," Raymond offered.

After Maggie's attempted disruption with her cell call,

she and Michelle were still waiting not knowing exactly what had transpired or if Don and Brandon were even still there at this point. The boys could have left in a different vehicle for all they knew. They had to just sit there and wait. Patience.

Michelle looked up into the rear-view mirror and noticed a dark figure in an overcoat ambling toward them. Michelle strongly advised Maggie, "Don't turn around. Here comes someone."

"Who?"

So what did Maggie do? She of course turned to look out the passenger window ANYWAY and saw a grinning, toothless, degenerate crankster in his fifties as he stared back at her.

Maggie gasped!

Even though the windows were up, they could still hear what the crankster asked and could almost smell him. "Hey, you girls lookin' for something?"

Maggie quickly turned to Michelle. "Are we looking for something?"

"No!"

Maggie promptly turned back. "No. We're not looking for anything!"

Then he asked, "You two wanna party? I got a rock." He grabbed his crotch and laughed.

"Ewe!" exclaimed Maggie.

"Get lost you sleazy pervert," said Michelle forcefully.

"Gimme' a ride and I'll smoke you out," he said to the both of them. Then he addressed Michelle about Maggie, "I think your friend here likes me."

Maggie shuddered and was ready to vomit. "Get LOST!" she screamed.

Suddenly, the neighborhood was lit up with flashing red and blue lights that were coming from Larry's location down the block, behind them. The toothless crankster saw the police, freaked and took off running. The girls turned to look out the back window at the scene behind them. Silhouetted by the glare of the police car's brilliant spotlight, they saw a car that they didn't recognize here in the dark with a lone figure sitting in the driver's seat.

"The police pulled someone over back there," Michelle assumed, "At least it scared that thing away..." She considered their situation further and said, "Maybe we'd better get outta here."

Maggie protested, "But what about Don?"

Michelle started the Suzuki. "We'll come back in a few minutes." She put it in gear and they drove off down the street, passing the bar and then turned right at the first intersection.

Maggie thought, *I bet Don 'll be gone by the time we come back. Even if I do lose him out here, I know he was up to something he assured me he wouldn't do.* Maggie wore a very forlorn expression and looked out the window as the lights went by while she fought back tears.


At the same time down the street, the police car with the flashing lights was parked directly behind Larry's car. The officer in the driver's seat had the patrol car's side spotlight trained on Larry's vehicle.

Larry was still watching through the camera's viewfinder and had no clue that he was under the scrutiny of the Oxnard Police Department. But he was about to find out. He saw Maggie and Michelle start their 4WD and drive away. He put the camera down quickly and was ready to start his car when the policeman in the driver's seat picked up the mic and addressed Larry on the patrol car's PA. "Open the car door, get out and keep your hands where we can see them," said the officer sternly.

Larry looked in his rear view mirror and was surprised and bewildered. He took his hand off of the ignition switch and said, "Fuck?!"

He did as he was directed to and opened the door, got out and stood there, motionless next to the open driver's side door.

There were two officers in the car and they both got out at the same time. The driver stayed behind his open door while he gave another command over the PA, "Keep your back to us and your hands up where we can see them. Don't reach. Walk backwards toward the sound of my voice."

Larry moved backwards looking over his shoulder slightly at them as he neared the trunk of his car.

"Stop there," said the officer with authority. "Now place both hands on the trunk and don't move."

The second policeman walked over and started to pat him down. He asked Larry, "Do you have anything in your pockets that's going to stick me or poke me or cut me?"

"No. What'd I do?" protested Larry strenuously.

The officer continued, "Do you have any weapons on you

or in your vehicle or any drugs?

"No. What've I done?" reiterated Larry brusquely.

At the police car, the first officer reported details as they were happening on the radio. "Dispatch. We have a lone male Caucasian outside of a car in the nineteen hundred block of South F as in Frank Street. California plate number, Three Ocean Nancy Charles Niner Eight One. Car occupied one time. Over."

The second officer asked Larry, "You the only one here?"

"Yeah."

"This is a bad neighborhood," he counseled Larry, "A lot of drugs sold here. What are you doing acting weird out here with that camera? You trying to look in somebody's windows with it?"

Larry sneered at the officer and quickly thought up an excuse as well as any other sociopath would have and answered, "Uh... I *was* spying on my girlfriend. She was parked up the street until you two showed up." He was halfway telling the truth. He was spying on them but neither one was his girlfriend. Of course, he had no girlfriends at all to spy upon. Just the unfortunate imaginary lovers in his head.

"Let me see your ID please, sir," prompted the second peace officer. Larry took his hands off the trunk, got his wallet out of his back pocket and handed it to the officer.

"Please remove it from the wallet, sir," said the cop perfunctorily.

Irritated, Larry angrily pulled the license out of it and shoved it at him.

The policeman said, "You can knock off the attitude. OK? There's no need to treat me like that, sir. I've been courteous to you. I expect the same. You can go home tonight, or you can go to the lock-up. It's all up to you and your demeanor here with me." The officer turned on his flashlight, directed it at Larry's ID and looked it over. He then looked up from the license at Larry with a faint smile on his face and said sarcastically, "Well, happy birthday, Mister Jenkins."

Larry smirked at him.

Without taking his eyes off of Larry, the cop outside minding him walked back over to the patrol car and handed the license to his partner to run for warrants.


Up the block at the dive bar, Don and Brandon walked out of the front door with the gun secreted in the bag that Don was carrying. They noticed the police lights down the block and came to a wide-eyed, screeching halt on the sidewalk.

"The cops are here," said Don fearfully. He started to act painfully suspicious as he looked around for an escape route.

After a second, Brandon responded with, "Hey, be cool ——I know—act like you just bought a hot gun."

Don looked at Brandon, then back at the police. It was then that Don thought he had identified the vehicle in front of the police car and asked, "Isn't that Larry's car?" Don couldn't believe it. "What the hell's he doing here?" After a second or two he then added, "He followed us??"

Brandon looked closer. "Yeah. It sure looks like it's him.

C'mon, let's go."

Trying to not stand out too much, they resumed walking to Brandon's car in the parking lot and got in. Don hid the bag with the gun under the passenger seat pushing it over a little hump on the floorboard, hoping to conceal it better should they get pulled over. But that wouldn't happen——Right?

Brandon started the car and pulled out to the driveway of the parking lot and stopped.

Don quickly suggested, "Let's drive passed them."

"Are you nuts? You just bought a hot gun."

Don implored, "I have to see if it's Larry."

"Trust me. It IS Larry," said Brandon. "We don't have to go down there."

"I WANT Larry to know that I saw him. Get going. We look suspicious just sitting here."

"Alright!" Brandon very reluctantly acquiesced. "Chill man. Jesus! I can't believe I'm doin' this shit!" After he turned on his blinker, Brandon cautiously pulled out onto the street and headed toward Larry and the police.


Larry waited by the trunk of his car as the second policeman returned from handing Larry's ID to his partner at the patrol car. Still standing by his open car door, the first policeman keyed the mic on the radio and asked, "Any wants or warrants on a Lawrence Edward Jenkins, date of birth today's date, in '75?"

Larry saw a car's headlights approaching. From Larry's

viewpoint, as the car passed by, he clearly saw Don and Brandon staring back at him. Larry turned into a seething volcano and shouted at them wildly, "Fuckers!!" He was fuming and stepped forward and shook his fist violently at Don. The second police-man grabbed Larry by the shoulder, spun him around and slam-med his face down hard onto the top of Larry's trunk right in front of Don and Brandon.

"Hey! That's it buddy," said the officer who immediately handcuffed Larry after they had passed the scene.

Don and Brandon turned left onto the first side-street hoping to vanish from the officers' view.

Just as the boys finished their turn off the street, Michelle turned back onto the same street, one block away heading the same direction as the boys were. She and Maggie slowly cruised by the establishment. They both looked into the bar's parking lot as they went by. No car.

"They're gone," complained Maggie.

"Sorry. I didn't want to hang around just sitting there. We might have been next."

As they proceeded, Maggie asked, "Are we going to drive right by the police?"

"Sure," Michelle said, confidently, "We haven't done anything wrong. Don't you want to see what's going on while we're here?" They continued onward toward the scene. As they drove by, from their vantage they saw Larry standing there in handcuffs.

Maggie's mouth dropped open. "It's Larry! What's he doing here?"

"That creep must of followed us," said Michelle disgustedly.

Larry saw them, too. The muscles in his face twitched uncontrollably as he clenched his teeth and stared intensely at the girls as they passed by. He shouted, "Fucking bitches!!"

The cop with Larry was fed up with his outbursts and shouted, "Hey! Hey!" The cop returned Larry's face to the metal trunk with a loud thud!

Maggie and Michelle saw it happen and laughed loudly. Loud enough for Larry to easily hear as they passed by. Michelle turned left up the same side-street that the boys used to leave the scene.

Larry simmered down after a few moments of staring closely at the fading paint on his trunk lid with the cop smashing his head against it. The first officer placed the radio mic back in the squad car, walked over to Larry and the other cop and stated, "He's clear. No warrants. Car comes back to him."

The second officer asked Larry, "OK now. Are you going to behave if I take these cuffs off?" as he let Larry stand upright.

After a moment Larry said, "Yes," placating him.

The officer unlocked the cuffs. His partner handed Larry's license back to him and walked back to the patrol car. The second policeman said, "You know, you're in a really dangerous part of town. You ought to be more careful. Oh, and next time, be a little more discrete with that camera of yours."

Larry obviously couldn't care less what the officer had to say to him. With that, he was free to go. So there went Larry— out—into the night...


Meanwhile, the boys made it almost five and a half miles. They had just completed their turn back onto the road that they entered Oxnard on from Ventura when suddenly, without any warning, Brandon's car was lit up by flashing reds and blues.

Brandon had a shocked look on his face as he looked into the rear view mirror. He was looking at five to ten. Don looked back at the patrol car's lights and thought, *This is it——*Again.

Brandon said to Don in a panicked, breaking voice, "Just be cool. Just be cool. Act normal and we'll get outta this."

Don's face had lost most of its color by that point and he looked as if he would hurl at any moment and asked Brandon, "Act normal?!" *What's normal about being pulled over by the police with a stolen gun in your vehicle that's probably been used in a homicide?* he thought to himself. *Normal??!*

Brandon put on his right blinker and carefully pulled over to the side of the highway. His car came to a halt and he put it in park and left the motor running. The cop's bright side spotlight came on and was flooding Brandon's face with light reflecting from his side mirror.

Brandon said, "Smile," to Don.

"What?"

"Smile. Stop looking like you're guilty, dammit!"

"Oh. Right." Don attempted a smile, pitiful as it was.

"OK," said Brandon, "Work on it a little more." Brandon looked back in the rear view mirror again and saw the deputy get out of his vehicle. Brandon said to Don, "Stop fidgeting and moving around."

Don worked on his smile.

Brandon looked at him. "I'm dead," he said quietly to himself, then looked back out his window.

The pot bellied, forty-five year old sheriff's deputy wearing a trouper style hat and thirty pounds worth of gear dangling from his duty belt, reached Brandon's driver's side window, just as Brandon rolled it down.

"Hi," said Brandon to him.

"Evenin', son," started off the deputy. "How y'all doin' tonight?"

"Just fine," responded Brandon attempting optimism.

Don squeezed out, "OK."

"I'm Deputy Freeman, Ventura County Sheriff's Department. Do you know why I stopped you, sir?" asked the peace officer to Brandon.

"No." He shook his head.

"Your license plate light is out."

"It is?!"

"Yup. Please turn your car off, sir," said the deputy who then asked, "Could I see your ID, registration and insurance please?"

"Sure," said Brandon as he shut off the engine.

The deputy bent down a little to look passed Brandon at

Don in the passenger seat.

"Hi," said Don again.

Don was smiling as good as he could, at least he was considering the circumstances. The sort of smile that would potentially break if he had to talk too much.

"Could I see your ID, too, please, sir?" he asked of Don.

"Absolutely." Don fished out his wallet and extracted said ID as Brandon was doing the same. Brandon reached over and opened the glove box and got out the registration and insurance papers and handed them to the deputy along with his and Don's ID.

The deputy said, "Thank you, I'll just check on all this and I'll be back in a minute or two."

Don's smile was frozen by now. The deputy turned and headed back to his patrol car. Brandon slowly turned to look at Don. Don was looking back at him, and, still smiling and trying to talk without cracking his face said, "We're going to jail because of a burnt out license plate light??!" he said as angrily as he could while still being quiet——and maintaining his smile.

"Shhhh. We haven't gone to jail yet."

*Yet*, Don thought.

"Just act cool," continued Brandon, "Stop thinking about what we have with us. It doesn't exist."

That seemed to help Don relax, at least a little, and he became more natural. *"These are not the droids you're looking for,"* came to mind for Don. It might all have been funny had they not had any contraband in their possession. And Don sat right on top of it. The one most proximate.

Three minutes of waiting while the deputy ran their ID's for warrants, seemed like an eternity, *plus* five years. Maybe time off for good behavior? Brandon saw the deputy get out of his car and head toward them.

"Here he comes," said Brandon.

"OK," as Don tried to speak without cracking the plastered on smile he was sporting.

Deputy Freeman came back to Brandon's window and asked Brandon, "Do you boys have any drugs or weapons on you?"

Brandon shook his head in earnest and answered, "No."

"Do you mind if I search your car?"

"Why do you want to search my car?"

"I'd been following you for a while and you were coming from a section of town here known for a lot of drug activity."

"Really?" Brandon squeaked out.

"Really," repeated the deputy. "Please step out of the car gentlemen and follow me back to my car."

"Uh———OK." Brandon looked at Don. Don looked HARD at Brandon. The two opened their respective doors and got out.

Another sheriff's vehicle, this time an SUV that had: "K9 – PLEASE KEEP BACK," posted prominently on its two back side windows pulled up behind the first deputy's vehicle and stopped. Don and Brandon were escorted back to the front of the first deputy's car as the second deputy in his thirties, got out of his car and went to the driver's side back door and got out his dog. Don and Brandon looked at each other.

Then, Brandon turned to the first deputy and asked, "Is this really necessary?"

"Like I said, there are a lot of drugs going through that part of town."

"But, what if I don't want you to search it?" pleaded Brandon in a calm tone.

"So you're not giving your permission then?"

"Uh, no. I mean, well, uh——Do I have to?" stammered Brandon.

"It's all up to you. But, because of the area you came from and the plate light being out that gives us probable cause to at least run a dog around your car and see if it alerts."

"It does? Just because we went to a crummy bar there?"

"Yup."

The second deputy had his dog by a bush alongside the road, "Break, break," he said to the K9 so it would urinate before the once over of Brandon's car began.

The first deputy asked Brandon again, "Are you sure there're no drugs or weapons in your vehicle?" He looked at Brandon like he was reading a book he'd read a thousand times before. "Honesty's the best policy with me, son. It'll get you a lot further."

Brandon reluctantly volunteered gratuitously, "There are probably a couple of roaches in my ash tray. That's it," as he shrugged his shoulders.

"OK," the deputy said. "That's a good start."

The second deputy had his K9 at the back fender of Brandon's car. He touched the back of the car and instructed the

K9 to, "Check, check," which it immediately started to do. He guided the dog around the back of the car and up the driver's side. The dog was sniffing the whole way. No response. Yet. "Good boy! Good boy!" said the deputy that handled the dog. They went passed the front of the car and started to go down the passenger side. Don's asshole was so tight it was almost twisted into a pretzel. The dog looked closely at the passenger door, lingered there for a moment and then proceeded toward the back of the car.

Don thought, *Whew,* to himself and began to relax a little. Brandon watched the whole affair and tried to maintain. Then ——the dog wanted to go back. Don's eyes widened. The dog got to the passenger's door, sniffed at it again———and sat. The boys did their best to not appear crestfallen. The deputy with the dog said, "Good boy! Good boy!" again to the dog, petted him big and then lead him away from Brandon's car as he gave the dog a treat.

The first deputy turned to Brandon and said, "Looks like he alerted to somethin'. That gives us the probable cause to search your car now."

Brandon said back to him in resignation, "OK," trying to be a cool cucumber and inadvertently put his hands in his pockets.

"Please keep your hands out of your pockets, sir."

He complied and withdrew them immediately. "Sorry."

The first deputy put on some blue nitrile gloves while the other deputy put his K9 back into his SUV and shut the door.

Brandon said, "It must just be those roaches in the ash

tray," hoping to throw the deputy off track. The second deputy came over by the boys to mind them as the first went on his quest for all the car's hidden places.

"Hi," said the second deputy to the boys.

"Hi," back from both in unison.

"So what were you two doing in Oxnard tonight?"

Brandon said, "Oh, uh, we just went to go see my cousin."

"What's your cousin's name?"

"Robert Mendoza," stated Brandon.

The deputy just nodded his head in silence as he looked at them.

Don ignored the deputy's inquisition of Brandon. Instead, he stared intently at the operation in front of him. The first deputy opened the passenger door, bent over and looked inside with his flashlight beam moving about the interior. He retrieved a few roaches from Brandon's ashtray and put them on the car's roof. Then he dove back in and looked like he was fishing around under the seats now. Don was doing his best not to scream and start running. He looked at Brandon who returned the concerned look, then they both looked back at the festivities before them.


Michelle and Maggie turned onto the same roadway to go back home.

"Look!" exclaimed Michelle as she spotted the boys with the deputy searching Brandon's car.

Maggie looked slack jawed at the scene as they went right

passed Don and Brandon standing in front of the first deputy's car.

Maggie said, "I can't believe this is happening!"

Neither Don nor Brandon saw the girls go by because they were so distracted by the search.

"Do you want me to pull over?" asked Michelle.

"NO! No way! I don't even know him!"

They continued onward, back over the bridge toward Ventura.

Maggie said, "I don't want to go right home yet. Can we go hang out somewhere for a while first so I can get my head together?"

"Alright, sweetie. Anything you need," responded Michelle in a motherly fashion, "I certainly understand." She reached over and patted Maggie on the shoulder, consolingly as she drove.

"This is all so much——so sudden." Maggie put her head in her hands as they neared the end of the bridge over the river.


As the first deputy searched, his hand went RIGHT OVER the gun, missing it completely. He then came back, groping blindly for one more search since the flashlight in his other hand couldn't shine in the right, or in Don's case, what would have been the very, very wrong place. Again, the deputy missed the bag with the weapon! He backed out of Brandon's car, folded the passenger seat forward and dove-in once more. He rummaged around the various fast food wrapper debris on the back floor board. So many articles of trash that the deputy didn't notice the straps on the bag with the gun sticking out from under the back of the passenger seat. Fortunately, it appeared that Don and Brandon were saved by an inept deputy. He backed out of the car, put the passenger seat back upright and shut the door, then picked up the roaches from the roof and brought them over to show Brandon. "This here's what you were talkin' about?"

"Yeah," said Brandon.

"It *is* legal now here but you really shouldn't be driving around smokin'."

"I understand," said Brandon.

The deputy asked, "Have you been smokin' out here tonight?"

"No," said Brandon convincingly.

The deputy responded, "You don't appear to be high to me." He then told Brandon, "I'm just going to give you a fix-it ticket. Those roaches must have been what the K9 hit on."

"Oh, OK," said a very relieved Brandon.

The deputy tossed the roaches on the ground, removed his gloves and said, "You have 45 days to get a new bulb in it. Just remember you might get pulled over again, though, so, don't wait the 45 days. If you do get pulled over again tonight, just show them the fix-it ticket I'll issue to you. Once you get a new bulb in it, come by any of our substations and any deputy can sign you off. Sound good?"

"Yeah, yeah," said an elated Brandon who tried NOT to sound, and look, all that elated.

The deputy stood there next to them, wrote out the fix-it ticket on the metal ticket box and handed it to Brandon. "Just sign here," he said as he pointed out the signature line. Brandon did so and handed it back. The deputy then gave their ID's and paperwork back, plus the ticket and said, "OK. You're free to go. Good night, gentlemen. Sorry for the inconvenience."

"'Bye," they both said and walked back to Brandon's car and got in, shutting their doors. They looked at each other and couldn't believe what had just taken place————and, just how close they had come...


Upon their arrival back in Ventura, Michelle asked Maggie, "Where would you like to go and hang out?" as they drove down the main drag in the Suzuki.

Maggie answered, "I just wanna disappear, that's what I wanna do. I feel so humiliated."

"No one knows about it, so no humiliation, right?"

"Brandon knows ALL about it!"

"Look," said Michelle, "Dillard's Coffee Shop is still open ——There?"

Maggie considered this a little too long. "Sure, I suppose... Yeah." By the time Maggie decided, they had passed it. Michelle flipped a U-turn, came back and turned into their parking lot which was mostly vacant except for four cars, two or three of which were probably employees' vehicles. The girls parked, got out, locked the grocery getter four wheeler of Michelle's and headed for the front doors.

They entered the vestibule, opened the second set of doors and entered the restaurant and saw that there was a "Please Seat Yourself" sign on a stand next to the hostess station. So they did, at a booth next to the front windows. The place looked like an old converted "Denny's" with the same cathedral ceiling and similar layout. The smell of coffee and pancakes and everything else on the menu was infused in the air with a soothing familiarity. To call it a "greasy-spoon" would be a needlessly derogatory pejorative since it really was a nice place. Most of their business was at breakfast and lunch with a smaller dinner crowd. After that, they would get a few stragglers til closing. There were two other occupied tables and one waitress. It was nearing 10 p.m. and, being a week night, things had slowed down. The restaurant wasn't particularly near the freeway, so most of the patrons were locals.

The waitress showed up with a pair of menus and placed them on the table. "Start you both off with some coffee?" she asked.

Maggie just looked at Michelle and kind of arched her eyebrows while she shrugged and smiled a little, making her dimples show. "What do you think?" she asked Michelle, then continued, "Just coffee?"

"Yeah," responded Michelle. "I think so."

"Cream and sugar?" enquired the waitress.

They both answered, "Yes."

"Be right back in a minute." The waitress confiscated the menus, headed behind the bar and deposited them in their receptacle.

"Don't feel humiliated by all of this, hon," suggested Michelle. "Even if Brandon knows, so what? He went out and did something illegal. You didn't."

Maggie just looked out the window.

"You know, I really fell for Don, and now this." She looked back at Michelle. "And after all of the heartache I went through years ago with someone else. Why can't I meet someone who's stable and normal and, and, and doesn't go out a buy a hot gun and lie to me about it?" She pounded the table causing the silverware to jump a little just as the waitress approached with their coffees.

She set them in front the two. "Just let me know if you want anything else——like some pie, for instance," she said suggestively to them with a hopeful smile.

"Thank you. Just the coffee 'll be fine," said Michelle.

"OK. Thanks." And with that, the waitress withdrew and went to the cash register at the hostess station and met one of the parties that was leaving so they could pay their tab.

Maggie dumped the third little pseudo "cream" cup into the black sludge coffee. "It's gonna take a lot of sugar, too, to make this palatable," she said.

"They're probably closing soon from the looks of it so I doubt they wanted to make another pot full just for us."

Maggie agreed, "Don't blame 'em."

There was a long silence as Michelle doctored her coffee, as well, to make it appetizing enough to consume. Of course, they really weren't there for the epicurean delights found within a coffee shop. They were there to escape——for the time being.

166

To let Maggie recover and vent before she went home to face...
whatever.

Michelle tried to console Maggie by reaching across the
table half-way to Maggie's hands and grasping them. "Sweetie,
it'll be OK. I'm sure of it. This will all work out somehow."

Just then the waitress returned and saw them holding
hands.

Michelle realized it looked a little gay and quickly withdrew her hands from Maggie's.

The waitress said, "That's OK," and showed them her
wedding ring. "My 'husband'——is a *woman*. So I got no
problem with it. You're cool with me."

Michelle quickly and defensively said, "I, uh, no. I mean
we're not——we're just best friends."

The waitress said, "Oh, OK. No problem." She winked an
obvious, over-the-top wink at them, put their bill face down on
the edge of the table with two mints and walked away.

After she was out of earshot, Maggie quietly said, "Great.
Now everyone thinks I'm a lesbian, too, on top of it all."

"Everyone who? There's one other table and they're at the
far end of the restaurant."

Maggie explained, "I'm not homophobic or anything, I
just don't want someone thinking that *I'm* gay. That's all..."

"I know," said Michelle.

Things quieted down for a while as they nursed their
beverages. As she became misty-eyed Maggie said, "I really did
love him. But now——now I don't know what to think."

Trying to give Don the benefit of the doubt, Michelle of-

167

fered, "For all we know they didn't get one. He could have changed his mind once they got there or the deal fell though."

That appeared to help Maggie a great deal. She suddenly clung desperately to the possibility that nothing *did* transpire. That he hadn't gotten anything there in Oxnard. No successful gun deal. A little, "I hadn't thought of that," smile appeared on Maggie's face. The first signs of any optimism whatsoever on her part in the last two hours had arrived.

"Maybe you're right," as Maggie readily and suddenly came around to the possibility and agreed. "We——I was just assuming that he had gone through with it... Maybe he had second thoughts... Maybe he nixed the whole deal and they left there with nothing... Maybe he felt bad and does love me enough *not* to go through with it after all." She looked as though a second wind had filled her sails. Hope sprang eternal.

"Well, let's hope that's what happened tonight," said Michelle. "There's every chance that's what did happen—— nothing. Nothing at all."

The waitress walked nearby carrying a box of set-ups to put on the tables for the next day's breakfast shift. Maggie hailed her, "I think I will have a piece of pie. Do you have any cherry?"


Brandon's car entered Don and Maggie's apartment parking lot and came to a stop near one of the sets of stairs which lead up to their apartment.

Don said to Brandon, "Thanks for setting this up for me.

Remember you can't tell anyone."

"Duh."

Don fished the bag with the gun inside from under the seat and looked up at his apartment. "I don't think Maggie's home from the movies yet. My apartment's still dark." Then Don added, "I know I was pretty pissed off at you earlier, but, it all worked out, and——I'm sorry."

Brandon said, "Hey, I understand. I'm pissed off at myself for not checking the damn car first, but, yeah, it all turned out OK, I guess." Then Brandon added, "Don't forget about me when all the shit goes down."

"I won't. If I can get it into work successfully tomorrow, I'll let you know what I've come up with as a plan."

"Cool. See ya tomorrow."

Don opened the door and exited. "Thanks again," he said to Brandon in parting as he shut the door. Don walked around the car and headed up the stairway. Brandon reached the second exit from the apartments as Don got to the second floor walkway and headed toward his front door. He got the key out and started to put it in the lock, then stopped and put his ear up to the door to listen in case she was home after all. No sound. Don slipped in the key, unlocked the door and entered feeling like everyone in the world outside was watching him and KNEW what he had in the bag he was toting. He shut the door and leaned against it for some time, so overwrought by what he had just skated-on-thin-ice through.

At first he was thinking, *Where in the hell am I going to hide this that Maggie won't find it?* Good question. He hadn't even considered that until then. He went into the bedroom and looked around. *She's all over the place here. I don't know where I could hide it in here that she wouldn't stumble across it.* Next, he went into their bathroom and looked around in there at hiding places. Only problem was, there really weren't any. She might find it by accident.

Fiester walked by and meowed at Don. Don asked him, "Where would you hide it?" Fiester stopped and looked at Don as though he had an answer for him. "I know," said Don jokingly, "At the bottom of your cat box." Fiester walked away and entered the bedroom. So, Don followed him back into the bedroom just in case Fiester was trying to suggest somewhere that he would hide something. Fiester jumped up on the bed and laid down. Don asked, "Under the bed?" Fiester sat there looking at him. "Good try. It's a waterbed. Nowhere under that. Thanks though."

Don walked out to the living room and looked around. Again, the same answer. There was no place out there either that she wouldn't encounter it by chance. Same thing for the kitchen. At that point Don simply gave up and plopped down on the couch, still with the bag in hand. *The only place left is my car,* he thought, *and with my luck it would get stolen out there tonight.*

On top of all he had gone through this evening with Brandon he felt very guilty about deceiving Maggie. The one he loved. So much so, that he constantly pestered her to get married. As more time there on the couch passed in the dark, there was more time to think. More time to realize that she probably already knew from his comments and actions leading up to her leaving with Michelle tonight. He thought, *Maybe I should just tell her. Tell her and get it over with. There's no point in trying to keep something like this from her if I really do love her...* And he did. More than any woman he'd ever known. He couldn't lie to her about this anymore. Then he figured, *I just have to find some way to explain it to her, to get it through to her, that we really* do need it *to save our lives. We have no choice now* because of *Larry.*

Don opened up the bag, withdrew the gun and placed it in the center of their coffee table——for all the world——and Maggie to see. No more secrets from Maggie. Never again after this. He set the bag on the floor and sat there keeping the weapon company while he thought about what he could possibly say to her to smooth things over. Yeah, right! He brooded, *Would she ever trust me at all, ever again?... Will she leave me over this? I wouldn't blame her. I'd be pretty upset if she lied about something as big as this to me.* He sat there ruminating further, *I'll just come right out and tell her the truth when she comes home.*

He looked at the clock on their wall just above the TV. 10:37 p.m.——*She should be home any time now,* he thought. His only hope was to try to reason with her that he was only doing this to save their lives. All he could do now was wait. Waiting on pins-and-needles. Waiting to find out if he had thrown it all away, or, if she would actually listen to his reasoning. He had only the best of intentions. "The road to hell is paved with good intentions," as the quotation says. The only hope Don had *was* hope. Time would tell if he was right about Larry and what he had assured everyone that the crazy man was capable of. Don really, deep down, didn't want to be right. He didn't want that in any way. He was only being prudent, he thought. Then, he heard a car enter the parking lot below. He drew a deep breath and let it out very slowly. *That's probably them,* he thought. *My life would be so empty without her.* His eyes became misty and he wiped them with the palms of his hands and sat there——— waiting. Waiting to find out his fate. With Maggie, that is. Who knew about the next day or two at work.


Michelle drove through the apartment's parking lot splashing through some irrigation water running off the flower beds. One of the residents was on his apartment's deck barbecuing steaks on a small Hibachi for a late night meal.

Michelle pulled into one of the parking spaces, stopped and turned off the four wheeler. She asked Maggie, "Do you think he's gotten back here yet?"

"Maybe. If he's not in jail already. I doubt they'd be driving all over the place if they'd gotten a gun———if they even did."

"Well, you'll find out soon enough. Let me know tomorrow at work," said Michelle.

Maggie said, "Maybe you're right after all, and he didn't get one... Maybe..." She smiled a little, grabbed her purse and opened the car door, then stopped and looked back at Michelle. "Thanks for helping me tonight. You're the only person I could ever trust with something like this." Something like this. How many other people have to deal with, "Something like *this.*" Very few. Very, very few in fact, she would have wagered.

"Hey, you're my best friend," Michelle said, "I'm glad to help out. I'm just so sorry this is happening to you... 'Night."

"'Bye," said Maggie as she stepped out and shut the door.

Maggie crossed the parking lot and went up the steps as Michelle departed the lot. *"Something like this,"* Maggie continued to think, *Why am I embroiled in "something like this?" I'm a good person. I never do anything wrong or illegal. I've never even gotten a parking ticket! And now look where I am.* She got up to the second floor and noticed the lights were off in her apartment and thought, *I guess he's not back yet. And it's getting late... Oh, I hope he's OK.*

She approached the door to their apartment with great trepidation and stood there for the longest time as she stared at it, not knowing what to do. What to do? Afraid to open the door to find——Don with a gun——Don in jail——Don shot and injured, or————Don with no gun at all. She took a deep breath and attempted to compose herself. *Let's get this over with,* she thought to herself. What awaits?

Don was still sitting on the sofa in the dark. Maggie unlocked and slowly opened the front door. As she did, a shaft of light from a street light outside illuminated the revolver on the coffee table like a spotlight focused on a performer on stage. She caught sight of it, and, with both a disgusted and disappointed look, stepped inside and shut the door behind her. The second wind in her sails, that maybe he didn't get one, had suddenly ceased to billow the sheets and all of Maggie's hopes had instantly been dashed on the rocks of despair once she caught sight of the gun. It was not the case that he'd had second thoughts and *did* love her enough *not* to do something like that. There was a protracted silence while she remained by the door. After what seemed like an eternity of quiet she said, "So you actually did it, didn't you?"

"I had to. What choice do I have? I have to assume that Larry means what he said."

"Michelle and I followed you to that bar in Oxnard tonight."

Don was totally shocked to hear that. "You did??" After he thought a second, he asked, "Oh, no. You didn't tell her what I was doing, did you?"

"Yeah——I did."

"Great! Now she knows... Why did you say anything to her about it?"

"I had to tell her why I wanted to follow you tonight," she said. "What else was I supposed to do?"

"You could have lied to her and said anything else but that!"

"Lies! Lies! Lies!" Maggie said disgustedly. "That seems to be the only thing you know lately..." She felt this was suddenly becoming a pattern with Don. He had never been like this before.

Of course, in Don's defense, he had never been hunted before, either. Changes your perspective a little.

"How much did you pay for this... thing?" she demanded.

"Two hundred. Cash."

"And I suppose you got it out of OUR account?"

He looked down at the floor and sighed. "Yes."

"That's nice!" That pissed her off even more, if that were

possible, that he'd used THEIR money for that——"thing"——
on the coffee table.

"I'm sorry," he said.

"Yeah. Whatever..."

After another silent moment or two, Don asked, "So, you
two followed us there?"

"Yeah. And Larry followed us," added Maggie.

"We saw him, too... So, he followed *you two*?"

"Yeah... At least I think he did, anyway."

Then Don said, "We assumed he followed us."

"He was parked right behind where we were sitting outside that awful looking place you went to," she responded.

Don postulated, "Looked like the police had him pulled
over for something."

She said, "We couldn't get over seeing him in handcuffs."

"He didn't have any on when we went by."

"I wonder what he did," speculated Maggie.

"He could be in jail right now," Don supposed.

"You're lucky *you're* not in jail right now!" she retorted.
She walked over and set her purse and keys down on the bar,
then went over and sat on the far side of the couch from Don. He
was on the left side of the couch, Maggie was on the right side,
with the gun on the coffee table between them, like the wedge in
their relationship this whole thing ended up being.

She looked disapprovingly at it and asked sarcastically,
"Are we just going to leave it on the coffee table?——Is it a new
knick-knack?" as she dealt him a sidelong glance.

He didn't respond to her. The two of them sat there and

stared at the gun. More time went by, wordlessly, between them.

Don said, "I feel very badly about lying. I'm sorry the gun upsets you... I know I'm doing the right thing, though."

"Do you??——Its only use is to kill."

Don turned to look at Maggie and countered, "And to defend."

The two sat in silence once more as they both stared at the revolver. The item that cleaved their, until now, serene and secure relationship. Things had been really good between them. Too good, perhaps. If it's too good to be true...

This was their first real relationship test. And what a super duper doozy for starters this was! Can't get much more extreme and drowning in betrayal and lies over such an ominous thing as this. It was a little worse than not putting the cap on the toothpaste or placing the toilet paper roll on backward.

"I just can't get over that you lied to me," said Maggie.

"You lied about where you were going tonight."

"No I didn't!" she protested, "We *were* going to the movies until we saw Brandon drive right by us and then saw you leave with him. When I saw that, and with the way you've been acting, and the things you've been saying I knew something was up for sure. *That's* when we changed our plans. I had to find out if you were going to——And you did."

"Oh... I'm sorry. I just assumed..."

She cut him off, "You assumed A LOT!"

"You shouldn't have followed me to that sleazy neighborhood."

They both looked at each other.

She folded her arms and crossed her legs and kicked a little nervously with her leg over and over trying to subdue her agitated emotions. She said, "Well, you had no business there, either," then added, "Plus we saw the two of you pulled over by the police on the way back home!"

"You did?"

"Yeah. Went right by you. I was so worried about you. I didn't know what was going to happen, and if you got arrested, if you'd tell them *that I knew* about all of it. You've put me through hell over this!"

"I'm sorry, Maggie," he said slowly with an almost not quite sincere tone to it.

"Did they search Brandon's car?"

"Yeah."

"And they didn't find it??"

"No. It was a miracle."

"No shit!" She thought a bit more and asked, "Why were you guys stopped by the police?"

"It was the Sheriff's Department."

"What——ever!" she said annoyedly, "Sheriff's Department then!"

"Brandon's car had a license plate light that was out."

Maggie was shocked, "So——you almost went to jail over a light being out?! Just because of a light?! Didn't that wake you up to what you're doing?!"

He stupidly asked, "Why are you giving me such a hassle over this?"

She laughed involuntarily and then asked rhetorically,

"Really??!"

"Look, I'm doing this for our protection. I'm only going to keep it around for a few days."

"I don't need that kind of protection, thank you very much," she said defiantly. She wanted nothing to do with this crazy harebrained scheme of his, even though she had already been sucked into it as an innocent bystander by association for simply having knowledge of his plan. "I could be an accessory because I new about this!" she said angrily. "Why did you put me in this position?!"

They both looked back at the gun and resumed their silence. More awkward time passed, then Maggie theorized, "And what if you get caught with it at work?... You don't know what this gun's been used for."

Don turned to Maggie. "At least we'd have a chance."

Maggie looked over at Don, "If you're so damn afraid of Larry, why don't you just take some time off or call in sick? I'm going to work though. I don't think anything's going to happen." Semi-confident, she was. It was like trying to convince yourself that a sure event, such as, the sun coming up tomorrow, *some-how wasn't going to happen*. Most of the time, statistically, she would have been correct in her assumption/hope that all would be well and Larry would just ride off into that psycho sunset never to be seen or heard from again. But this was——Larry ——they were dealing with. Not one of your run-of-the-mill psychopaths.

"What?" he asked.

"You heard me. You take some time off and I'll go to work

like normal."

"I'm not going to leave you there alone!" insisted Don.

"You're going to loose your job or get arrested for nothing!" she warned.

"At least we'll be alive. Larry's more dangerous than you think. He followed us tonight, didn't he?"

"He's just a horny guy with no social skills," as she tried to play it all down.

Don questioned, "How can you trivialize everything he's done? He hasn't even been fired yet and he tried to kill me today. Twice! Isn't that enough proof for you that I'm right?"

Groping and flailing about for excuses she said, "You're exaggerating what happened!"

"Are you kidding me?! You weren't there!" Don couldn't believe it. She wasn't there to see the look on Larry's face when he was attacking Don. It was beyond belief.

Don had done and said everything he could do to convince Maggie that they're facing certain death if they don't do something to protect themselves. It was true that he should have gotten a firearm a long time ago, legally, but that was where the intersection of procrastination and denial had dumped them out in the desert, tied to a chair with no way home. Don said, "I'm just sorry I didn't get a gun the correct way before all of this. I have no choice at this point." But even beside that, Maggie had always been vehemently against guns as long as he had known her. Even in the most ideal circumstances, she would never accept nor tolerate him having a gun of any sort. Another reason he hadn't gotten one. And now——it's too late. He was painted into a corner by his own inaction, knowing full well what the possibilities were.

She looked back at the gun, "You're risking everything over this stupid gun. Your job, prison, or maybe even your life. Have you *really* thought this thing through?——I think your actions are impulsive and irresponsible——aaand I'm not so sure I want to marry someone like that." Hoping that would be a bargaining chip to bring him to his senses.

"I *have* put a lot of thought into this," stated Don confidently.

"HA!" she exclaimed.

More silence ensued. He turned to look back at the gun, "You'll change your tune when Larry charges in with a gun and starts shooting. I don't like the thought of anything happening to you——Or me——Hell, the company can't stop him from harassing you and stalking you, what makes you think they can stop him from shooting you?"

He had a point there. A little crack in her reasoning had formed that she quickly had to gloss over to maintain. She couldn't admit it because if she had, her edifice might begin to crumble.

"Sane people don't bring guns to work," she stated as evidence.

"And Larry's NOT sane, is he? We don't work in a sane world. It looks like we can't count on anyone but ourselves for our ultimate survival."

"Well, I'm beginning to question *your* sanity." Then she added, "You're as crazy as Larry."

Don rolled his eyes at that one.

Maggie was serious, though. Sane people don't go out and purchase an illegal firearm and then smuggle it into their gun free workplace.

Things became quiet again as they both stared at the weapon on the table before them. Don turned to face her, "Now listen, I've worked out a plan...

Maggie interrupted, "You're taking this thing too far. Nothing's going to happen." She began to stand up but Don grabbed her hand to stop her.

"Look, just hear me out," he pleaded.

She sat back down, "Fine. Go ahead," she said dismissively as she folded her arms again.

"If you hear gunshots, stay in your office and hide. I'll be there as quickly as I can."

"I'm not going to stay in there!"

He explained, "If you're out in the hallway, he could come around a corner. If there's no place to run, you'd be dead!"

"Well, what about you running around out in the halls?"

"I'LL have a gun. You're safer staying in your office. Just lock your door and get under the desk til I get there."

She turned to look at him, "And what if I'm not in my office? What then?"

"If you're very close to your office, go there. If you're closer to an exit, get out and head for the front parking lot and I'll get there as soon as I go by your office and check for you."

They both looked at the gun again. She asked, "Are you going to keep it loaded?"

He turned to her, "No. I'll just throw it at him! Of course I'm keeping it loaded. If anything goes wrong I'll be in trouble whether it has bullets in it or not. There probably won't be enough time to load it before it's needed. It has to be loaded—— I'm planning on keeping it in the bottom desk drawer so I can get to it fast."

"If something goes wrong," she said, "Don't tell ANYONE that I knew about this."

"I won't. I promise."

She huffed and said, "Your promises..."

Maggie looked away toward their front door, exhausted of things to say and arguments to make. He wouldn't budge. She tried.


At roughly the same time, outside of a Ventura neighborhood bar, Larry pulled up in his car and parked in the shadows off to the right in the establishment's parking lot. He sat there for a moment, then took a swallow from a bottle of whiskey that was in a paper bag. He'd been at it for a while now, getting drunk ever since he was accosted by the Oxnard boys in blue. Larry thought, *I would have killed those fuckin' cops! Deader than shit! They were so lucky I didn't have my gun with me ——Dead!!* His face muscles involuntarily twitched, as they seethed under his skin. While he sat there musing to himself about his misadventures with authority both earlier today and this evening, a red Mazda caught his attention. The car parked underneath a pole with a bright light on top of it next to the front of the bar. It looked like a thousand insects were flying around the light, swarming it. Two slightly tipsy women in their twenties got out and shut their doors. The driver locked the doors with her remote. Chirp.

Larry leered at the two giggly females as they walked across the crunchy gravel toward the front door of the bar. In Larry's mind, he had their clothes completely off of them before they got halfway to the front door. He was almost having mental orgasms as he spied on them and couldn't contain himself. The psychosexual sicko was writhing and hunching uncontrollably as he watched them make it to the entrance, open the door and go inside. When they opened the door you could hear the loud music from within, then as the door slowly closed the sound diminished to virtually nothing until the door shut.

*I'll have 'em cornered in there*, he somehow thought in his fantasies. Only in his fantasies, though. He was almost ready to go in there and take over the scene. Larry took one more gulp, screwed the cap on tightly, then stuffed the bottle under the seat. He got out of his car and semi-staggered to the entrance. Larry was absolutely plastered at this point and he wasn't done yet.

Inside, the sound of a cue stick hitting a cue ball with a loud crack was enough to compete with the booming jukebox. Two men in their thirties were in the midst of a pool game against each other. A couple in their forties was dancing to the music coming from the jukebox. The smoky bar room was dimly lit by the light above the pool table and various colors of neon beer logos adorning the dark green painted walls. Walls that

183

looked like various drinks had been flung upon them over the bar's lifetime and never quite got cleaned off all the way, leaving hints of drippage streaking them here and there.

The two young women that just arrived had seated themselves on stools at the bar and were still giggling about anything that they encountered it seemed.

Larry stood in the entrance and surveyed the scene. In short order, he spotted the girls that he was stalking sitting at the bar and made a bee-line for the open stool next to them. He plopped down there and was obviously and uninhibitedly feasting visually off of the two. The two knew this but ignored him.

The crusty old female bartender set down two napkins and two bottles of beer in front of the tipsy women who were lighting up cigarettes. Apparently this was another smoking prohibition scofflaw joint.

The song faded out and the couple that was dancing sat down at a table where they had left their bottles of beer.

The bartender slid an ashtray closer to the girls and asked Larry, "What can I get for ya?"

He slurred, "I'll have what these two super hot babes are having."

Larry looked them up and down as though they were already nude and chained to a basement wall, each with a ball gag taped in their mouths.

The two girls looked at each other and cracked up, then the first woman asked the other, "Got any quarters left? We need music around here." Her friend dug in her purse for quarters as Larry received his beer and paid. No tip, of course. He reached into his pocket and pulled out two quarters and said to the girls, "I've got a couple of quarters here." He held the coins up but didn't hand them over. Instead, he stared, transfixed psycho-sexually at them.

After a couple of seconds of waiting, the first one asked him, "Well, are you going to give them to us or what?"

With that, Larry suddenly slammed the quarters down on the bar with a loud bang, right in front of the women, startling them.

"You can have 'em if you tell me your names," as he reeked of booze. So many fumes that, if you lit a match by him, he'd probably burst into flames.

She turned to her friend and said, "He wants to know our names." She turned back to Larry, and, as she picked up the quarters said sarcastically, "I'm 'Thelma,' and this is 'Louise.'" The girls cracked-up, grabbed their beers and giggled their way across the room over to the jukebox, leaving pathetic Larry behind at the bar. Socially, ineptly, inanely oblivious to the joke, he actually thought those were their names and proceeded as such.

Larry sat there as his blood alcohol level rose steadily and watched as the two looked through the selections while he gulped down almost his entire beer convinced that they were both hot for him.

The girls were still huddled over the song menu on the machine's front, searching.

Then, "Thelma" suggested, "D-2?"

"No, F-4," "Louise" objected.

"OK, OK. F-4, D-2, aaand... B-13."

185

Larry shouted, "Bingo!" causing the bartender to chuckle.

The girls looked over at him, then at each other and began laughing at him again. They turned away from him and started to deposit the coins in the machine. Larry finished off his beer as the bartender showed up with a fresh one. He paid for it. No tip again.

"Thelma" punched in their selections. Larry picked up his beer and sauntered over to the jukebox and them. With all the regalness a dork could muster, Larry leaned on the jukebox just as a record began to play. The sudden blast of unexpected music made him jump wildly and he sloshed the beer about. The two girls looked at each other and deliberately turned away from Larry to laugh——again. He was so out of it he didn't realize that *he* was the butt of their amusement.

After they quit laughing, "Thelma" looked over at the pool players. She gently nudged her friend with her elbow and motioned with her eyes toward the two men shooting pool and said, "The one in blue is a babe."

"I kind of like the blond," responded "Louise."

"Thelma" took a drink of her beer and handed it to "Louise." "Here, hold this," she said.

"Thelma" then moved to the center of the dance floor and swayed her body back and forth to the rhythm of the music. "Louise" walked over to a table, sat down on one of the chairs and crossed her long legs under her short skirt.

The pool player that "Thelma" had the hots for was about to make a shot. He was looking straight down the pool stick, to the cue ball, to "Thelma's" curvy hips in her tight jeans as she moved suggestively to the music. She glanced over her shoulder toward the pool table to make sure she had his attention with her mating dance. Totally distracted by her, he made his shot and scratched.

His opponent said snarkily, "S'matter Bubba, mind not on the game anymore?"

"Hey, fuck you, man!" he said back.

Dismayed, "Louise" said to herself, "'Bubba'??"

Larry took his beer with him out onto the dance floor near "Thelma." He stared at her and tried to move his body to the music, but his rhythm was ridiculously off. Larry's eyes were glued to every inch of her body. She, and "Louise," were to be his conquests for tonight, he thought somehow in his wildest sicko dreams. He said to her, "Hey 'Thelma,' you sure are a good dancer."

"Get lost, creep!" she exclaimed.

Larry danced over to "Louise" and set his beer down on the table. "Don't you like to dance?" he asked her as he grabbed her by the arm and tried to drag her out of the chair, "C'mon 'Louise.' Let's dance!"

"Let go of me!" she yelled loudly and jerked away from him. "I don't want to dance! Especially with YOU! Leave me alone!"

Rejected, Larry abandoned his beer and moved back to "Thelma" on the dance floor. It was all starting to spin around for Larry, locked in his sexually backward trance. Her young, voluptuous, writhing body became too much for him. Way too much. He danced around behind her, as though now, in his sexually stunted, dysfunctional paraphilia fantasy, they were somehow going to have sex——right there, no less. He said to her, "Oooh, 'Thelma'!" Then, suddenly and uncontrollably, from behind he primally grabbed her by her breasts, one in each hand, squeezing them tightly. She shrieked loudly and kicked at him!

Bubba and his pool game opponent quickly headed toward Larry menacingly with their pool sticks, ready for use, to avenge his attack on "Thelma"——who ended up with the one that she had the hots for that night after all. Maybe Larry both, ironically, and, unintentionally did her a favor by introducing her in a sideways fashion to, "The one in blue..."

Don and Maggie's living room was dark. Maggie insisted that Don put that "thing" in a drawer in the kitchen. They had hardly said a word to each other after their couch conversation had concluded. Mostly one word answers of, "Yes" or, "No." Neither side would concede to the other. It was trench warfare with no yardage gains or losses, only stasis stagnation, minus the concertina wire and trench foot. She was so mad at him she couldn't cry over it any longer. Or, so she thought.

It was late and Don was zoning out. Maggie was brushing her teeth in their bathroom at her vanity. Don entered the room and stood before his vanity and looked at himself in the mirror next to Maggie. She finished and as she used a towel she asked him, "Like what you see?" about his refection, then added, "What have you turned into? This obsession you have about Larry. You're not the man I've known for the last two years. This whole thing has changed you into——a stranger..." She hung up the towel and continued, "...to me."

Don looked downward, feeling ashamed but confident in his actions, even more so now. Their lives were at stake and this was no longer in the realm of the theoretical. Far more probable than possible he surmised. "I don't know what else to say to you, Maggie. I'm still the same person I've always been."

Maggie shook her head, no. "I don't know what to say either." At a loss for words. She exited the bathroom and laid down on the bed with her back facing his side of the bed. He followed her and laid down next to her and tried to put his arm around her, but she threw it off. Don sighed and turned over with his back to her. He considered saying something but thought better of it. *Maybe she'll come to her senses in the morning,* he thought to himself.

She had virtually the same thought as he did, simultaneously, but in reverse. *He might come to his senses by morning,* mused Maggie. *He'll have slept on it and in the morning he'll tell me he made a big mistake and begs for my forgiveness... He'll realize I'm right and we'll get rid of that thing somehow—— Have to make sure our fingerprints aren't on it anywhere though...*

She set the alarm on the clock, reached over and turned off the light on her nightstand. She laid there in the semi-dark riding a roller-coaster of emotions. Wanting to scream and start hitting him, and, alternately wanting him so badly she could scream. Sleep for her? Impossible. She was wide awake on the battle bullet train from hell.

On the other hand, Don's thinking for the night was fading fast as sleep snuck up on him and engulfed his conscious mind seamlessly flowing into hypnagogic dreams. Dreams of Larry waiting around every corner at work wielding a lightsaber ready to cut him and Maggie in half. Then, the lightsaber turned into a seven foot long, four hundred pound pipe wrench falling toward Don from high above and no matter where he tried to run, this "Wrench of Damocles," followed him until it was merely inches away.

He stirred a little, still paralyzed in dreamland.

Maggie on the other hand couldn't sleep if she tried. Not even if you held a gun to her head. How could she? There was one in the kitchen drawer. Her entire safe little world started to crumble away in only one day's time to where she had no idea what was what anymore. What did she really know? What, or, who did she trust anymore, other than Michelle?

She sat up on the edge of the bed. She didn't know why she did or what to do next. She just did. Maggie didn't know what to do with herself. It was like she was "Jonesing" for something. A way out. Anything. The "drug" of her former existence that she wanted back with him more than anything. So she sat there——silently. Externally silent. Internally, a cacophony of thoughts parading around like a circus of clown cars. And instead of clowns pouring out of the cars, guns came piling out, all shapes and types and sizes. Maybe she was dreaming?

Diving deeper into REM sleep now, Don was having more Larrymares. In this one, he saw Larry's face from when he drove right out in front of Don on the roadway so Don would T-bone

Larry's car. This time, in the dream, it was all in ultra slow motion. While Larry stared straight at Don, Larry's face slowly morphed into a hideous monster with horns and glowing red eyes, a maniacal smile and a bizarre echoey laugh, sounding distorted. No other sound. Not the screeching tires. None of it. Only the extremely surreal laugh.

Don involuntarily jerked slightly again.

Maggie laid back down and started to wonder if she really was asleep. Maybe she would be rescued by reality when she awoke from her nightmare any moment now. *The most elusive thing in the world here——was reason*, she thought. Hell is a place where there is no reason. She turned over and looked at sleeping Don and just stared at the back of his head for the longest time. If only she could open his cranial vault and tinker around with the synapses that went bad, thus correcting the situation at hand and causing him to be repelled by guns and violence. A kind of, "Ludovico Technique." A Clockwork Don.


Larry had a lot of alcohol that night. A lot a lot. He stood in his bathroom, in front of the basin on the vanity, grasped and turned off the hot and cold water faucets with a squeak once the basin was full and splashed water onto his abraded face which stung like hell. "Owww..." as he winced in pain. He looked at his reflection in the mirror and examined the scrapes and bruises on his cheek and forehead as water dripped from his face and plopped into the basin below.

"Fuckers," he quietly called them under his breath as

though they're still within earshot ready to inflict more damage and public humiliation upon him. He toweled himself off, looked in the mirror once more with his bloodshot, horizontal gaze nystagmus affected eyes, then left the spinning room for his spinning bedroom. Multiple encounters with the police today, but none occurred when he was driving around, *twelve* sheets to the wind. Amazing how it worked. By all rights, he should have been sobering up in a city drunk tank by morning. But elude them he did somehow.

Larry was clad only in his boxer shorts as he entered the bedroom. It was obvious that something more was brewing in his mind despite tonight's nonexistent perverted courting outcome. He walked over to the closet and pulled out a medium size, white suitcase with various scuff marks and dirty spots on it showing that it had been a lot of different places in the past. He laid it on the bed, groped under the mattress, found a key and opened the suitcase. Larry then sat on the bed next to it.

His demeanor changed abruptly as he looked into the suitcase and his eyes got big. He reached into it and removed two Barbie Dolls clad only in miniature leather G-strings and pointed metal bras. He removed the G-string and bra from one of the dolls. Larry rubbed the doll up and down on his crotch repeatedly while he enjoyed the sensation it was giving him, plus his having been the master of the helpless doll. While he did this, he asked the doll, "How do you like it, you little bitch?" Larry thrust the doll's head through the fly of his boxers, "Oooh, yeah, little whore." Beads of sweat popped out on his quivering upper lip as his head started to jerk up and down uncontrollably so he looked a little like a demented version of Max Headroom.

Next, Larry pulled a miniature, doll sized strap-on dildo out of the suitcase and strapped it on the other doll. These two captive dolls were real in his contorted mind. They were analogs for the two in the bar earlier who were meant to be his sex slaves. He held the naked doll up to his face and looked it in the eyes, leeringly, then laid it on his pillow face up and said, "You want me to fuck you, don't you? You're just like those sluts at the bar, aren't you?" He started to act like he was strangling the doll as his face reflected the sickness that spewed from his head. It was almost orgasmic for him.

After that, Larry took off his boxers. He knelt on the bed facing the doll, began masturbating and asked it, "You like that, don't you? You fucking whore." It didn't take long at all before Larry suddenly moaned loudly, then almost immediately ejaculated.

The poor doll's smiling face was splattered.

# THURSDAY

*MARK J. WILSON*

The sun had just crested the mountains in the dawn to the east of town casting long rays through the sky from them, and some spotty, dark clouds above. Clouds of foreboding.

Maggie laid in bed on her back and stared at the ceiling. She had barely slept at all. After all he went through yesterday, she didn't see how he could sleep. But sleep, he did. Soundly. Like a baby——with a .44-magnum. Every time she closed her eyes and drifted off herself, the slightest noise outside or from Don would bring her back to the reality she sought to escape from. *Has he totally lost his mind?* she thought to herself as he slumbered so serenely on his side next to her. *This whole thing is crazy.* Different thoughts of what to do raced through her mind like competing race cars as she laid there... *What to do? This can't be real*, repeated in her mind over and over like a tape loop. *I'm so glad I didn't tell him that I'd marry him. I can't stand being lied to. I've had enough of that in my life from before. He has to stop this——or else.* And she was dead serious.

She looked over at the night stand and the alarm clock.

6:47 a.m. Maggie turned on her left side and looked at Don. She saw him in a whole new light. And not a good one at that. She thought, *I just can't do this anymore if he's going to go sneaking around behind my back and doing insane, illegal things. I don't want anything to do with that. If this is how it's going to be——it's over.* Tears started to run down her cheeks. She had fallen in love with Don so hard, so head-over-heals for him. *Why does it have to end this way? Why did he have to do this at all and ruin everything between us? He ruined my trust in him. I had just gotten to the point where I really could let go and trust someone fully again——and now this——Never again.* She considered waking him and resuming the argument. But to what end? He was totally intractable on this, that was for sure. All the reasoning she put forth so far made no difference.

What to do?...


At the same time, it was deathly still in in Larry's darkened bedroom. He laid there asleep seemingly in the midst of a dream as his face subtly reacted to what he was dreaming about. No doubt something utterly disgusting, sick and offensive to most. He sneered and tried to speak, but couldn't. Suddenly the alarm clock went off like a bullet in the brain. He reared up in bed with a crazed look on his face, grabbed the unfortunate clock and hurled it against the wall as hard as he possibly could, silencing it forever as it shattered into little clock bits that rained down onto the floor.

Slowly the look on his face changed as he transitioned

from his former dream state into his twisted awake reality state of existence. "Fuck!!" he yelled loudly as he clenched his fists while his face looked like he would kill.

Shortly thereafter, Larry entered his kitchen clad in boxers, a dirty, stained T-shirt and socks. His hair was as messed up as he was. He dropped a couple of cherry Pop-Tarts in the toaster, started it and then walked over to a window in the living room. Larry opened a couple of slats of the blinds and peered out of the slit. He saw Albert talking to one of the neighbors. Larry couldn't make out what he was saying. After a few seconds of watching through the blinds, Larry saw Albert turn and point toward Larry's house. Larry instantly closed the slit and headed back to the kitchen just as the tarts pop.


Across town, John and his forty-five year old wife, Sharon, are dressed and ready to go as they sat together at their dining room table. He drank the last of his coffee and closed a travel brochure that he was perusing. Sharon, an investment firm manager, finished arranging paperwork in her briefcase and shut it.

"I still can't believe it," Sharon said, "This time tomorrow I'll be on a plane going to Hawaii with you."

He smiled and took her hand. "I can't believe it either. Our second honeymoon," he said to her as she smiled broadly back at him. They leaned toward each other and kissed then looked lovingly into each other's eyes until a large grandfather clock in their entryway chimed once.

"Gotta go," he said to her. "I love you so much darlin'."

"I love you more," she said, then she remembered, "Oh, and I did talk to Scott next door and they'll watch our house for us while we're gone."

"That's a relief," he responded.

They both stood up. She grabbed her briefcase.

"See you tonight," she said then they kissed again and looked at each other blissfully.


It was still dark in Larry's bedroom. A darkness that could never rival him though. He fumbled around looking for his trousers. He found a pair and started to put them on. He got them halfway on and realized they were the ones he got a huge stain on and never took care of.

"Shit!!" he yelled and was thoroughly enraged as he ripped them back off and threw them violently at the wall causing his eyeglasses to fly off of his head in the process. He threw the pants at the same part of the same wall with the divot in it from the alarm clock's departure.

Larry reached down and retrieved his spectacles, found another pair of pants and growled loudly to himself, nearly shaking he was so pissed-off. All this over just clothing.


Fiester was in Don and Maggie's kitchen and was rubbing himself against Maggie's legs as Maggie placed some dry cat food in a bright blue bowl. She bent down and placed the bowl in front of their cat as he quickly went for it.

"See, I haven't forgotten you. I love Fiester," she said to him as she petted him a couple of times. He purred loudly between bites.

She bent back up from her brief respite, her brief distraction from that, "thing"———and there entered Don from their bedroom carrying *her* tennis bag.

"That's MY tennis bag!" she exclaimed.

"I couldn't think of another way to get the gun into work. It looked too obvious in the bag I had it in last night."

She shook her head and laughed a little and said with a very angry, and at the same time, hurt tone, "I can't believe you're going through with this insanity. I just don't know what's come over you."

"Let's go or we'll be late," he said to her.

She just glared at him, then, reluctantly abided, shaking her head as she picked up her purse and walked toward their front door. No, he hadn't come to his senses when he awoke as she had hoped. *This just can't be happening*, she thought.


Larry was bare from the waist up. He rolled open the closet door and saw only empty hangers. He slammed the door shut, hard, nearly derailing it and walked over to the laundry basket, picked it up and dumped the contents out onto the bed. He scanned the pile, picked up a tan shirt and sniffed the armpits. Then, after a couple seconds of thought, he sniffed his own armpits, as well. Satisfied, he threw on the wrinkled shirt anyway.

On any given day, Larry's attire resembled the mismatch of dumpster dive garb. The best in homelesswear. He looked like his mother the circus sideshow clown dressed him. It really didn't matter what he wore though. Larry would've looked like shit in a gold suit.


Brandon looked at his reflection in his bathroom mirror as he finished making sure he looked decent. Suddenly, he froze and stared at his image wondering if he'll ever come home again after today. He studied the reflection of his face closely, as though he had a premonition of things to come, then, after a few moments he looked away and exited the room bound for the outside world.

He slammed his apartment's front door and flew down the steps and over to his car. He jumped in, started it up and revved the engine. Then the stereo cranked up. Boom! Boom! Boom! He put on his sunglasses, looked in the rear view mirror at himself, liked what he saw (he also liked that there were no police cars in his mirror) and backed out of his parking space.


Michelle rolled a wheeled garbage can down her driveway to the sidewalk and set it down into the gutter for its pickup later that day. She waved to her neighbor, Jonathan, who was just about to get into his car. He set his coffee travel mug on the car's roof, fumbled with his keys and said, "Hi," to Michelle. He hurriedly opened the car door and got in, having already forgotten about the coffee.

"Hey, Jon. Don't forget your coffee," she said as she pointed to his drink left on the roof.

"Oh, thanks. Duh!" Instead of getting out and retrieving his beverage like he should have, he tried to do it from his driver's seat with his hand reaching up to the roof and knocked it off the car onto the driveway anyhow, splashing it everywhere.

Michelle shrugged her shoulders, "I tried."


Akino stood on the steps of his front porch with his thirty-five year old, Japanese-American wife, Suzanne, and their two children, a five year old boy and a ten year old girl. He hugged and kissed his wife, then bent down and kissed the 10 year old on top of her head. He mussed up the hair on his son's head after which his son annoyedly straightened it back out.

"Call me right after you see the doctor today," he said to his wife.

"OK. I will."

"And don't worry," he continued, "We can afford another baby. We'll just have to." He smiled proudly, turned and headed down the steps and along their walkway to his car as she and the kids looked on.


In the front parking lot at Hunter, Slater drove up in an old Chevy pick-up with a patchy paint job that had seen better days, parked and got out. He folded the seat forward, reached behind it and got his jacket which was covering his black 12 gauge pump shotgun. Seven shells in its magazine, ready for—— whatever might unfold. Better to be prepared. What Don had warned him about yesterday weighed heavily upon his mind all night. The instinct to survive is a strong one. This company's premises was a "gun free zone," but, that really means "open season" on employees. It's only gun free to the law abiding. If they couldn't care less about killing their coworkers, they really don't care at all about having a weapon on site against the company's make-believe, false sense of security policies. Apparently it didn't stop Don in his attempt at security and self preservation, and now, Slater as well.

Slater pushed the seat back into place, shut the door and locked it. He stood there next to the vehicle, put on his jacket, zipped it up and walked away toward the building. Larry was the prime freak in a circus sideshow which featured an employee shooting gallery. And that was what Slater was going to do his level best to prevent.

It also really troubled him that *no one in management* bothered to let him know the gravity of the situation that could unfold here. He would never have known, had Don not spoken up and tipped him off. If you know that there was at least some remote possibility, you should inform others. Especially the ones that were there to protect the masses from THE ONE. As he approached the front of the building, he thought to himself, *Hopefully, I'll never run into this guy and he'll just go away and leave everyone here alone.*

Don drove down the freeway in his maroon with white racing stripes, late-model Camaro. Maggie was his passenger. The windows were half open and the breeze blew her hair about which was back-lit by the golden glow of the morning sun.

She was sitting halfway in her seat and the other half backed up to the passenger door——watching Don. She stared at him, someone now strange, that she had never really seen before. Someone she lived with and had a relationship with. Don noticed her as she stared at him. He looked over at her and then back at the road. She continued her gaze. Don looked at her again and smiled. Maggie looked away, out the windshield, at the road ahead.

Don obliviously asked, "What?"

She had an involuntary, nervous laugh. "'What?'..." she repeated as she shook her head then looked out the side window. Maggie thought, *'What?'——What a ridiculous question—— Oh, nothing really. Nothing's wrong at all at the moment—— We just have an illegal weapon in our car, that's all! No biggie!*

She then looked back at him and asked, "Are you speed-ing??"

"Oh," he looked at the speedometer, "I'm about ten over I guess."

"Well, slow down dammit! Maybe you've forgotten, you have an illegal gun in here and I don't want to go to jail!"

"Oh, yeah," as he immediately slowed down to the speed limit——minus five miles per hour, and started looking all over for the police that he was sure would be right there———when you *didn't* need them. "Thanks," he said.

She had a disgusted laugh, then said, "Not doin' it for you..."

A few minutes later they reached the sprawling engineering building's front parking lot, entered it and proceeded to Don's usual parking place.

He switched off the ignition and Maggie immediately reached for the door handle to bail. Don turned toward her, "Wait," he implored and took her hand as the office building loomed in the distance through the windshield. He asked, "Why can't you believe in me?"

She thought, *Why can't I believe in you? Seriously? You lie to me and then go out and spend two hundred dollars of OUR money on something that I find to be abhorrent. 'Believe in YOU?'*

Maggie silently glared at Don then pulled away from him. Without a word, she got out of the car with her purse, slammed the door and stormed off. He grabbed the tennis bag with the gun, shut the door and ran to catch up with her.

Maggie headed straight for the building. Don was hot on her heels and caught her by the wrist and they stopped. She looked at his hand on her wrist, then back up at him and he let go. She then continued, and he did after her, at a fast pace toward the building.

Don begged, "Can we talk about this at lunch?"

Maggie said tersely, "I think I have plans with Michelle."

She entered the front doors first, letting the door shut in Don's face as he got to it. He then opened and entered the door trying to catch up to her. She got to the guard's desk and stopped. The guard wasn't there at the moment. As Don caught up with her, she looked down at the bag, then at Don, then at the vacant guard station. They started moving again and the two entered the main hallway. He tried to kiss her good-bye but she turned and walked away from him in a huff.

"'Bye...," he said pointlessly as she headed down the hall toward the stairway, ignoring him completely. Don looked down at the bag he was holding and his shoulders drooped noticeably. He turned left and went toward the drafting department.

A few moments later, as Don carried the tennis bag he rounded the corner leading to drafting and saw his supervisor, Louis, ahead at the coffee station. Louis looked up and noticed Don approaching. Don slowed his pace, somewhat panicky at having run into his boss during his gun running operation.

Louis greeted him with, "'Mornin' Don."

"Uh... Hi, Louis," he said back, trying to act natural. He was getting a lot of experience at it.

Louis said, "I'll be by your office around nine o'clock."

"Oh, yeah. Around nine. See you there." Don passed Louis and continued toward his office.

Louis enquired, "You takin' up tennis?"

Without thinking through his answer in the slightest, Don immediately said, "No," then looked down at the bag and then back at Louis, "Oh, yeah... A little." Don thought, *That was a stupid thing to say!* But it was too late. It had been uttered.

This struck Louis as an odd thing to say, but, not having a suspicious nature, he thought nothing further of it. Louis will eventually put two and two together, but it will be after the fact. Fortunately for Don, Louis was satisfied with Don's weird non sequitur of an answer as Louis had more pressing matters to deal with that day——or so he thought at the time.

Of course, Don was certain that Louis's, "X-ray vision," *and*, "psychic abilities," revealed that there was actually a gun in the tennis bag minus a tennis racket.

Don finally reached the refuge of his office. He stuck the key in the lock, anxiously opened the door and rushed inside, quickly shutting and re-locking the door behind him. The blinds were closed and the office was dim. He leaned against the door and heaved a huge sigh of relief, looked at the bag in his hands, then proceeded to his desk. There, he switched on a desk lamp then sat in his chair. He opened the bag, took out a T-shirt from the bag and opened the bottom desk drawer. Don carefully and cautiously unfolded the T-shirt revealing the gun. He pointed the weapon downward at the floor, opened the cylinder and checked that it was loaded then delicately closed it back into the gun with a click. He then tried to rotate the cylinder to make sure it had seated properly. It had. It wouldn't budge. He carefully placed the gun in the drawer, covering it with two software manuals, then slowly closed the drawer so as not to jostle it in any way.

Don turned off the desk lamp and sat back quietly in the dark. He closed his eyes and began to wonder if he really *was* crazy and Maggie really *was right*. By then it didn't matter. At that point it was too late. The gun was there for better or worse ——hopefully for the better in that equation.

Don thought, *I know I'm doing the right thing... I hope...*
Nagging doubts persisted. Better safe than really, really———
really sorry.

Running into Louis certainly wasn't something he had
expected nor bargained for. He thought it would be a smooth
operation getting it safely and discreetly to his office. And there
was his boss———standing between Don and the gun's eventual
hiding place in his lower desk drawer. But, it all worked out it
seemed———to that point anyway. *I just have to not think about it
being here*, he thought, *Just forget it even exists for now. Try to
act normal... Forget I have a hand cannon here against company
policy. One that's probably been used in a homicide... Stop
thinking about this!... Clear my mind.* Yeah. Easier said than
done.

After a few moments of quiet solitude and recovery from
his jitters over the clandestine activity and guilty thoughts and
actions, he stood, went over to the window and opened the blinds
allowing the morning light to flood in.


Maggie reached her office, unlocked the door and went in.
She put her purse away in a desk drawer, sat down in her chair
———and came face-to-face with the picture of Don on her desk.
At first, she glared at it, then, gradually, she looked as if she
would start crying at any moment and fought the tremendous
urge to do so. She reached over and turned the picture face down
on her desk. She rolled her eyes and shook her head as she
leaned back in her chair and stared at the ceiling.

*I have to put myself first, ahead of this craziness,* she thought, *I'm going to have to find an apartment and move out. I can't live this way with him.* She sat up in her chair and jiggled the mouse to wake up the computer. She went to her favorite search engine and typed in: Ventura Furnished Apartments for Rent, and hit enter. A huge list of apartments popped up in the area. After she looked at a couple of them, she started to have second thoughts. *Maybe I'm being too hasty. Maybe I should give him a second chance,* she thought. *What, and have it, or something else happen again?... Uh-uh. No way!* Back to looking at the listings. And, after three more, she stopped again with the same quandary——another chance for Don? She was so unsure and so torn, that she was tied up in an emotional knot, unable to make any rational decisions. She opted to not pursue the apartment avenue, at least not then anyway. She decided about one thing though, and that was to find Michelle and let her know that he really did do it.

She stood up and walked out of her office.


Maggie came around the corner of the hallway near HR and ran into Brandon. He had a package that he was delivering to someone nearby.

Maggie said, "Hi, Brandon," in a somewhat suspicious—— I'm really pissed-off at you, manner.

Not immediately knowing what to make of her odd vibe greeting, Brandon said, "Hey, Maggie. How goes it?" Then he started to wonder if Don told her about it. He still had no idea that she and Michelle had followed them. Then, he became more stilted and said, "Uh, well, gotta go and deliver this."

Maggie smiled subtly at him and nodded her head. "Yeah," she said slyly without coming right out and saying, "I know damn well what you two did last night!" but saying it, just the same. They both continued on their separate ways, with him thinking, *Shit!—She knows!*

Maggie went passed Michelle's office and didn't see her. She walked around a bit looking for her and passed by the shredder room. There was Michelle doing away with documents galore. The industrial size document shredder produced a loud mechanical hum. Several large, clear plastic bags of shredded documents and blueprints lined one wall. Michelle stood at the throat of the high-volume shredder, feeding it as it crunched up the paperwork turning it into unrecognizable irreconcilable debris.

Maggie entered the room as Michelle looked up and saw her.

"Hey," said Michelle.

Maggie said, "Hi," dejectedly.

Michelle finished the last of the documents in the boxes and turned off the shredder. The room was orders of magnitude quieter now. Michelle quietly asked, "I've been waiting to hear what happened."

Maggie began with, "Well, he DID get one last night and brought it in to work with us this morning."

"Shhhh..." cautioned Michelle who then said in her library voice, "You'd better keep your voice down. Go shut the door," she advised.

Maggie hadn't thought about her voice carrying down the hallway and went over and shut the door quietly. Suddenly paranoid, Maggie thought, *That was brainless of me. Hope nobody heard me.*

Michelle asked her, "So they didn't get arrested last night with that gun on them?"

"No. He said the police missed it when they searched Brandon's car! So, they didn't get arrested. He said they got pulled over for a license plate light that was burned out!"

"Are you kidding me? They risked all that with a burned out light?!"

"Yes!"

"They were damn lucky!" Then Michelle asked, "So, it didn't matter what you said to him about it?"

"Nope. He wouldn't listen to reason. It was a waste of time talking to him. He's convinced he has no other options and that the company isn't doing enough to protect us. He already had his mind made up."

"So, he just went ahead and got one?" asked Michelle.

Maggie said, "Yes—But he did fess-up to me when I got home and told me about it... He had the thing laying on the coffee table when I got there."

"You're kidding? On the coffee table?"

"Yes!"

Michelle tried to look on the semi-bright side of it and said, "Well... at least he did tell you about it. There's something in his favor."

"Very little something. I had hoped, really hoped that you were right and he didn't get one, but..." Maggie fell silent.

Michelle said, "I can't believe he would actually do something like this. This all seems so unreal."

"I don't know what to do," said Maggie of her predicament. "I never thought I'd have to deal with anything like this ——Ever."

Michelle consoled, "Don't worry. We'll figure something out." She thought for a moment or two, developed a wry smile, then turned and looked at Maggie. "I know. Did he tell you where he was going to hide it?"

"Yeahhh?..." said Maggie with some apprehension at not knowing what was coming next.

Michelle revealed her plan of action, "Well—maybe you'll just have to sneak into his office and take it."

Maggie was astonished that Michelle would hatch such a scheme and said, "I could never do something like that. You're as crazy as Don. What do I want with it??"

" *You,*" Michelle explained, "don't want anything with it. You're getting it out of Don's hands. Take it to your office. Once you have it, call me. Then we'll sneak it out at lunch."

As Maggie shook her head she said with immense reservations, "I don't know about this."

"Think about it," Michelle reasoned, "What else can we do without getting him some sort of trouble? It's away from him for safe keeping, then it leaves the building."

After a short while Maggie said, "OK... We get it outside ——then what? If we go anywhere we have a hot gun with us.

What about that?"

"I dunno..." Michelle then furthered their plan, "Maybe we toss it in a dumpster nearby work. How about that? We just have to make sure no one sees us and that we wipe all of Don's and your fingerprints off of it."

Maggie slowly warmed up to the plot. "That sounds reasonable." As though *any* aspect of this contorted state of affairs sounded, "*reasonable.*" Maggie continued, "I might be able to pull it off if you create a diversion of some sort... Why don't you call and tell him he needs to come down to your office?"

Michelle pondered this for a second or two. She posited, "I could tell him he needs to sign some papers, or——or something."

"That should give me enough time."

Both nodded their heads at each other in silent agreement. That was to be their plan. The plan to save Don's ass, or, so they thought. So long as it didn't get their asses in legal hot water subsequently. They would have been taking a gigantic chance in carrying that out, but what else could they do? Sit back and watch and see what happened? Bide their time? That was always an option, though not one they'd considered in their haste to right the wrong. There was always the chance that they could be dragged into all of this simply for knowing about it and not reporting it to the company *or* the police.

Notifications of continued employment, or severance packages and standing in the unemployment line began happening at 9 a.m. sharp that day. The plan was to notify all of the affected individuals within two hours, well before lunch. Tension was thick in the air in the office building where so many were on continued employment pins-and-needles. No one was walking around out in the hallways gossiping or wasting their time——the company's time. Not today. It was all business as the department heads went door-to-door handing out good news for the ninety percent, or bad news, for the not so lucky ten percent of the company's workforce. A little more in some departments, a little less in others. Most knew their fate already based on their work ethic or how little "work" there was in their work ethic. Most bosses took note of dilly-dallying staff. The ones who spend their days around the water cooler or coffee station in nonproductive frittering of time. Why have two employees that waste half of their time when you can get the same productivity from one diligent servant?

John shook hands with Akino in Akino's office after reassuring him that he still had his job. "Once again," said John to Akino, "Congratulations. Glad you're still on board here."

"Thanks. Me too. You don't know what a relief that is..." And, relieved Akino was with their third child on the way. Akino got a more serious look on his face, then looked over at the wall between his office and Larry's. "I suppose you're going to see *him* next?" as he tilted his head in the direction of the crazy man's office next door.

After a second or two John reluctantly answered, "Yeah——and I ain't lookin' forward to it, that's for sure."

Akino nodded in sympathy with John.

215

John moved toward the door, "Guess I'd better get it over with," he said. John opened the door and turned back to Akino, "Anyway, keep up the good work." He smiled at Akino and exited his room bound for——whatever unknown awaited him next door.

John traversed the short distance between offices, tapped on Larry's open door and entered, shutting the door behind him. Larry was sitting at his desk, waiting. "Hi, Larry," John said to him with great apprehension.

Larry asked, "So, what's the news?" He was psycho-certain in his delusions that he would never be fired. They wouldn't dare! It would be the only excuse he needed. The only thing holding back the flood gate——of blood.

"Larry," John said somewhat nervously and matter-of-factly, "I'm sorry but——we're goin' to have to let you go." He handed Larry an envelope. Larry was totally dumbfounded by this news and his mouth was left gaping open. "This is your severance," John continued, "I'm sorry. That's just how it is." That, "just how it is," was intolerable to Larry. It was utterly discordant with his oddly wired brain. Circuits were melting down, akin to a nuclear reactor, and there was no stopping it now. No containment vessel. No unringing of the death knell...

Larry looked at the envelope in total disbelief. He leaped from his chair, startling John, and began to wave his arms and pace back and forth. "I can't believe you're doing this to me! I've worked hard for this goddamn company!"

John directed, "Effective immediately you are to collect your belongin's and vacate the premises."

"I can't believe this shit! You can't do this to me! My boss is a piece of shit and this company's the asshole!" Larry stopped pacing and stared at John. "This is all Maggie and Michelle's fault isn't it? That's what I get for being nice to those bitches! Don't take this job away from me," begged Larry.

Akino was sitting at the desk in his office listening to the yelling coming from Larry's office next door.

Larry walked over toward John.

"You just don't get it Larry. You're fired. It's too late. There's nothin' you can do about it."

The last fraying cord hanging on tightly in Larry's synapses just snapped and the truly, unambiguously homicidal Larry emerged from the depths, sprung from a bottle, not to be put back or reversed. With undisguised contempt, Larry got right in John's face, just inches away. John leaned back slightly and Larry's speech took on a calm, ominous tone, "'Nothin' I can do about it', huh?" That was the last thing you would ever want to say to a person like this. To them, it's a dare. A challenge to be enjoyed. Knock the chip of my shoulder. The only problem was that it would be knocked off by a .45-caliber slug.

What little confidence John had drained away and was replaced by visceral fear. "What are you talkin' about Larry?"

Larry stared intently at John with a faint smile on his face, "There's plenty I can do about it."

"There's nothin' left for you to do but leave," John repeated.

"YOU, don't get it, do you?"

"Look Larry, I don't want any trouble." John headed for

217

the door and Larry followed him, like a group of hounds tracking a fox.

Larry declared, "This job was my whole life. I have nothing left to live for."

"I'm just doin' my job," John put forth as he opened the door to retreat.

As he became bellicose again, Larry exclaimed, "I'm gonna do a job on YOU!" If people thought he was scary before, they hadn't seen ANYTHING yet.

John left Larry's office and did his best to ignore him and started down the hallway toward his own. Larry followed him and stopped in his now, former doorway and yelled at John, "At your birthday party, I was just practicing!! I'll be back!! This time it'll be for real!!" The "Time Bomb" had begun ticking.

Akino stood in his own doorway listening.

Larry turned and saw him.

Akino quickly ducked back into his office, slammed the door and locked it.

John was so distressed by this interaction that he had to take a break from notifying his staff about their status. He passed by the rest of his employees' doors, went straight to his office and shut the door. He leaned against the door and tried to replace what had just freshly occurred with Larry by thinking about his trip with his wife to Hawaii tomorrow——It wasn't working. After a few minutes solitude, he had cleared his head a little and resumed his task at hand. John thought there was no point in reporting this to HR. He was no longer an employee. John opted not to call the police either. It seemed pointless. But

218

the more he thought about it, the more he realized he had to do something to document Larry's threats and also what he had tried to do to Don the day before.

John walked over to his desk and briefly stared at the phone. He then opened one of their corporate directories, located a phone number and called the Ventura Police Department.

After a couple of rings a female officer answered, "Ventura Police Department, is this an emergency?"

John said, "Uh, no. I just needed to report some threats one of our employees was makin'."

"Can you please hold?"

"Sure," said John compliantly. There was no hold music. What would it have been if there was? The theme from COPS or Live-PD?

After about a minute a male policeman picked up. "Hello, this is Detective Harmon. What's going on?" he asked.

John said, "Well, it's probably nothin'. This is John Stanton at Hunter Engineerin'. One of our employees was just terminated here and made threats to my life and supposedly tried to kill another employee yesterday."

"Ehh. Better to be on the safe side. We take things like that very seriously. I'll send someone over shortly to see you and take a statement."

"Thanks. I'd really appreciate it."


Enraged, Larry set a large, empty cardboard box on a chair next to his desk. With his arm he swept everything except the phone off the top of his desk with a loud crash into the box.

Next, he dumped the contents of the two desk drawers into the box and threw the empty drawers on top of the desk with a loud bang, knocking the phone receiver off the hook. The dial tone began.

He yanked open the file cabinet and pulled out some files and tossed those into the box. Larry reached for his two framed degrees, ripped them off the wall and flung those items into the box as well.

He grabbed his jacket off the back of the chair and put it on. The dial tone stopped as he picked up the box and exited his office without looking back. The recorded Operator message began, "If you would like to make a call..."

Slater had barely returned to his guard station when the phone there rang. He picked-up, "Guard station, Slater."

On the other end was the ever on-the-ball, Rankin calling. Rankin said, "I got tied up and didn't get a chance to call yet. Anyway, we'll need an escort out of the building for the employee I pointed out to you. Jenkins." Anytime Rankin opened his mouth, incompetent came out of it.

Slater answered, "I'll go up there right now."

"Thanks," said mister inept.

Slater hung up. He went to take a drink of his now cold cup of coffee and opted not to, then he looked up the office number for Larry on his copy of the floor plans. Room A327. Third floor, 'A' wing. He took the walkie-talkie off of his duty belt, put it on the charger strip, got a couple of fresh ones and went over to Jennifer. He handed one of them to her. "Here," he said, "In case I need to contact you, here's a walkie-talkie." He pointed to the "Push-To-Talk" button. "Just press this button when you talk and release to listen."

"OK," she said as she nodded her head.

And off he went on his escorting Larry out of the building mission.

At the same time, Don was working at his computer drafting station when his supervisor, Louis, entered the room. Don looked up from his work.

"Hey, Don," said Louis, "Great news. You've still got your job."

Don stood up and they shook hands. Very relieved, Don said, "Thanks, Louis. I was a little worried."

Louis patted him on the back, "What? You didn't have anything to worry about. Looks like we just keep on doin' what we're doin' here." They shook hands again. Louis continued, "I've got to get going. I still have the rest of our group to talk to ——Oh, we're having a department meeting tomorrow at 10. See you there." Louis went to the doorway.

Don repeated, "Thanks again."

"Sure thing Don." Louis went out the door to his next employee.

Don looked down at the newspaper in the chair next to him. The headline: "DEATH IN THE WORKPLACE..." blared at him. He still, even now, was trying to convince himself that all would be good with Larry. That he would take the news of his firing and simply move on. *Right*, he then thought. Concerned over Maggie's employment fate, he picked up the phone and dialed her extension but got her voice mail.

"Hi, you've reached Maggie Kimball in purchasing. I'm either on the phone or away from my desk..." Don hung up the phone and left his office, bound for hers.


Sunlight was coming straight in the front entrance. Larry entered the lobby from the hallway carrying his box. Jennifer looked up, saw Larry with his box and even though she knew the answer already, asked snidely, "Going home early?"

Her remark caught him off guard and forced him to laugh.

"Yeah————But I'll be back."

Her smile instantly washed away into a look of concern.

Larry opened one of the double glass front doors and walked out into the bright morning light.


At the same instant, Slater got to Larry's vacant, ransacked office, looked around and said to himself, "OK. A little late. Looks like he already escorted himself out." Slater held up his walkie-talkie and keyed the mic, "Jennifer, this is Eric. Are you there at the front desk?" he asked.

She picked up her walkie-talkie and said, "Yes. I'm here."

Slater asked her, "Have you seen Larry Jenkins in the last couple of minutes?"

"Yeah. The creep just left with a box of his stuff."

Slater nodded, "That's good. Thanks. Out." He thought, *At least he is gone, with no incident——yet...* Slater left the room knowing if something was going to happen, it would more likely be sooner rather than later.

Maggie stood next to the desk in her office. Her shapely body was silhouetted by the window she was facing. As she dialed the phone, Don showed up. He liked what he saw and leaned against the door jamb, taking it all in. After a short while, he said, "Hi there."

She turned around, "Oh, there you are." Don entered and went over to her while she hung up the phone. She said, "I was just trying to call you. I still have my job."

"Me too."

They embraced reflexively.

"So," he continued, "you're not mad at me anymore?"

With that, she pulled back from him and asked, "Who said I wasn't?"

A few minutes later, after he left Maggie's office, Don caught Brandon just as he was coming out of the mail room with his cart on his first floor run. "I'm glad I caught you before you left," said Don somewhat loudly so Brandon could hear him over his MP3 player.

Brandon turned off the player, yanked out his earbuds and asked, "Still have your job?"

Don said, "Yeah. What about you?"

"Cool. My supervisor said I'm stayin', too."

"Congrats," said Don. Then he nodded with his head in the direction down the hall and said quietly, "Let's go over there." They walked down the hallway a few feet to a section where there was a long passage without any offices on either side and stopped there so they could conspire further without discovery.

Brandon looked around and asked, "Did you bring it?"

"Yeah. I brought it in this morning with me. I hid it in my bottom desk drawer in case I'm dead and you needed it."

"Does Maggie know you got it?"

Don nodded his head.

"You told her??" asked Brandon. "I just ran into her and she acted like she knew all about it!"

Don said, "You'll never believe this——She followed us to Oxnard last night."

Brandon was thoroughly shocked. "No shit?!" He looked around again, fearing he was being too loud. Then, more quietly, "No shit? I didn't see anyone following us in the rear view mirror."

"Her women's intuition was on fire or something I guess and she didn't trust me. Your call didn't help either. I think it was the icing on the cake for her."

"Sorry, man..."

"So, she *and* Michelle tailed us. They even saw us after we got pulled over. Drove right passed. I didn't see 'em."

"Me either. Man..." Brandon thought a second and asked, "So does Michelle know too?"

Don nodded affirmatively, "Uh-huh. At least I think she does."

"Man, this ain't good."

"Anyway. I came to tell you the plan..." said Don just as the door to their main frame computer room opened up a few feet away and one of the company's male IT nerds exited while engrossed with something on his smartphone and walked in their direction. Don tried to cover as fast as he could and improvised, "Uh, so, I just wanted to let you know that——I'm waiting for that second package from Fed-X. You guys in the mail room lost the first package and I had to spend extra money to get it re-shipped."

"Oh, uh, sorry," Brandon ad libbed, "I'll make sure..."

He was interrupted by the IT employee as he passed by, "Hi guys."

Don said, "Hi," back to him.

Brandon said, "Hey, what's up?"

"Nothin'," the IT nerd replied as he continued away down the hall, still focused on his device.

Once he was far enough away, Brandon asked, "What'd you have to make me look like I'm a screw-up in front of the dude?"

"Sorry. It was the first thing I could think of quickly."

"What? That I'm a screw-up?"

Frustrated, Don admonished, "No——Listen——Do you wanna hear the plan?"

"Yeah. Sorry."

Don said, "If you hear shots, and you're anywhere near Maggie's office, go directly to her room and wait there. I'll be going straight to there from my office with the gun."

Brandon asked, "What if I'm by an exit?"

"If you're closer to an exit, bail out and go to the front of the building and we'll meet you there."

Brandon nodded in agreement and said, "Oh—Yeah. OK ——Yeah, cool."

Larry arrived at home, pulled into his driveway and parked. Next door, Albert was watering his lawn with a sprayer. He waved at Larry.

Larry got out of the car, reached back in and dragged the box of his belongings from work across the seat to him and said to Albert, "Every time I come home, you're out here. You live out here?"

Albert looked at his watch, "You're home early."

"I took the rest of the day off," grinned Larry as he slammed the car door shut. "In fact, I'm on vacation. And I'm planning a little hunting trip."

Larry entered his house and shut the front door. He proceeded to the kitchen and set the box on the counter next to the sink where he began unpacking it. First, he removed the file folders and threw them aside. Next, he pulled out his two framed degrees and glowered at them, "All those years——for nothing." Larry disgustedly tossed them into the garbage which shattered the glass with a loud crash against the metal can.

Then, he opened one of the kitchen drawers. Inside the drawer was a gray .45-caliber, semi-automatic pistol. He picked it up and set it by the box on the table. Larry reached up to a cupboard, opened it and withdrew a small box then set it next to the gun. He opened the smaller box which contained five extra magazines for the weapon and a couple of boxes of ammo. He placed the gun in the box with its accoutrements and shut it.

Maggie sat at her desk talking to Michelle on the phone.

Michelle said, "Well, I'm ready, are you?"

"As ready as I'll ever be, Maggie replied. "What am I going to say to Don when he finds out?"

"Tell him you did it for his own good. I don't know, we'll worry about that later."

Maggie said, "Let's get this over with. Call him now."

"'Bye," said Michelle.

Maggie hung up the phone. She turned her purse upside-down and emptied it into one of her desk drawers. She snapped the purse closed, hung it over her shoulder and headed out the door on her sabotage operation.

Michelle then dialed Don's extension and after a couple of rings he picked up.

227

"Hello. Don Thorp."

"Hey Don. Michelle."

Don was at his desk sipping coffee from a mug. "Oh, hi," he said, then mischievously asked, "So, how was the movie last night?"

Michelle was thrown for a loop not knowing if Maggie told Don that they followed him, so, just in case, she tried to not blow their cover. "Oh, uh, interesting," she answered, hoping he'd leave it at that.

Then Don asked, "What was your favorite part?"

At first she stumbled for an answer, "Uh... I liked the part... uh..." Then after a second a faint smile appeared. She abandoned her deception and said, "I liked the part where the two guys went to buy a stolen gun. That was *my* favorite part."

Don was speechless. He looked down and shook his head.

"You still there?" asked Michelle.

"I'm here——So Maggie really did tell you?"

"She told me what she thought you were up to last night. We had plenty of time to talk while we were trailing you. But I didn't know you actually got it until today when I saw her earlier."

"Listen, you can't tell anyone about this," pleaded Don.

"I won't. YOU just make sure you don't tell anyone that I knew. Fair?"

"Fair," he conceded.

Michelle now had the phone cradled on her shoulder as she fiddled with a bracelet. Feeling no guilt over it, considering what Don had done and was doing, she began her ruse, "The reason I called was there was a mix-up on your dental insurance forms. They had to be redone. Can you come over to my office and sign them? I have to send 'em off right away before the deadline." She had no problem carrying out that deception, it seemed.

"OK," he answered, "Be right there." He hung up and sat there for a minute pondering whether or not she would keep the secret. *She'll probably keep her mouth shut,* he thought, considering she was also complicit, in a way, by staying mum about his efforts. Don stood up and headed toward his door.

Maggie crept up to the corner leading to Don's hallway and peeked around it. She saw Don exit his office and walk away down the hall. She waited for him to disappear around the corner then quickly made her way to his office, looked around to make sure no one was watching and slipped inside. She closed the door, locked it and moved promptly to his desk. Maggie opened the drawer and moved the manuals aside. With a thoroughly revolted look on her face, she removed the gun, barely holding it upside down by the grip with the tips of her thumb and index finger as though it was a slimy, stinking turd and secreted it in her purse. It was all she could do to keep from being nauseated, so repelled she was at being forced into handling the weapon.

Don arrived at Michelle's office, knocked on the open door

229

and went in. Michelle was working at her desk.

"Hi, there," he said to her.

"Hey, Don. Here're the forms." She handed the paperwork to him. "Just sign and date them where the X's are." She gave him a pen and he leaned over and signed them on her desk. He handed the pen back and detached his copy.

"Thanks." Don decided to go fishing about her and Maggie's lunch plans, "So, what are you and Maggie doing at lunch today?"

"We're... Uh...," as Michelle quickly groped for an answer, "It's a surprise."


Just as Maggie reached for the doorknob to make her getaway from Don's office, a knock at the door startled her. Her eyes darted about as she tried to remain calm while clutching the purse tightly.

In the hallway, standing at the door, was Louis holding some paperwork with some specifications that Don needed for a project.


Don stood in front of Michelle's desk, continuing to press her about their lunch plans, "Is it something Maggie is doing for me?"

"Yeah. I don't want to spoil her surprise for you."

Oh, how surprised he will be.

"Well," as he gave up, "OK..." Don started for the door

then stopped, "Oh, did you find out if you still have a job, yet?"

Michelle said, "Yes. Fortunately—What about you?"

Don said, "Same here. Anyhow—'Bye," and left her room.

Michelle breathed a sigh of relief as she rolled her eyes.


Louis tried the doorknob on Don's door but it was locked. He got the keys out of his pocket——thought for a second—— then put them back in his pocket and walked away down the hall.

Maggie had an ear pressed tightly against the door and heard Louis walk away. After a few seconds, she cracked open the door and peeked out. The coast was clear and she made her escape.

Don rounded the corner into his hallway just as Maggie barely ducked out of sight down a different hallway.

He entered his office and sat down at his desk. Don picked up his coffee mug and looked inside, made a face then set it down on the desk. He reached for the bottom drawer where the gun was residing, until recently, and started to pull it open but changed his mind and opened the top drawer instead, tossed in his copy of the dental form and closed it. He got up, grabbed his coffee mug and headed out the door.


Larry sat in his chair in the living room with pen in hand writing on a yellow note pad. It was to be a suicide note, if you could call it that, to whomever would be interested after the fact. His last utterances memorialized for posterity.

The floor surrounding him was littered with yellow crumpled up previous attempts at distilling his twisted and rambling thoughts. Thoughts of revenge, of multiple vendettas against those who had wronged him. They must pay, he thought! And pay they all shall. He gave up on another writing, grunted loudly and ripped the page off the pad, waded it up with a vengeance and threw it over his shoulder. Larry began rocking forward and backward a little and stared straight ahead while he loudly tapped the pen on the note pad. So scrambled were his thoughts, they were almost impossible to condense into anything vaguely resembling a coherent thought. But still he would press on, writing another version, and another, and another. And for what? In the end, who would really care? Maybe the families. Maybe the survivors————if any...

Michelle looked at her watch, thought Maggie should be back by now, then picked up the phone and dialed her extension.

The phone on Maggie's desk started ringing just as she flew into her office and shut the door. She reached across the desk and picked up, "Hello."

"Hey, it's Michelle. Did you get it?"

Maggie continued around her desk and stuffed her purse into the bottom desk drawer.

"Yeah, I just stuck it in a drawer." Maggie had suddenly acquired Don's paranoia, certain that the whole building——NO ——ALL of Ventura, somehow knew she had the gun hidden in HER desk now. She went so far as to look out the window up to the sky for the police helicopter. Maggie asked, "Do you hear any helicopters?" as she peered upward.

"No...?" said Michelle with a quizzical look on her face ——then realizing Maggie must think that she's being surveilled, Michelle, with a raised eyebrow continued, "Don't worry. Everything's going to be fine, hon. We'll get it out of here shortly."

Michelle's words gave Maggie some solace. "OK," she said, then looked back out her window up at the sky again, anyway.

The floor in Larry's living room was now littered with several of Larry's crumpled notes. Larry walked toward the front door and opened it holding the gun box in his hands. He turned and looked back at the house one last time, then exited, closing the door behind him. His footsteps outside faded away.

Don was seated at his computer drafting station with his back to the door as he worked. He heard a soft knock at the door, turned to look over his shoulder and saw John finishing the knock. John stood there with a Ventura Police Department officer in uniform. Don swiveled his chair around 180 degrees to face them. His desk was between the two at the door and him and he reflexively looked down at the drawer with the gun in it and then, with a guilty look on his face, quickly looked back at them. "Uh, hi. What's up?" he asked very nervously as he still pathetically tried to act nonchalant.

John said, "This is Corporal Rhodes. I called the police to report what happened with you and Larry yesterday, plus he threatened me today, too." Corporal Rhodes was a tall, very buffed out African-American in his thirties with a thin mustache.

The corporal said, "Hi, Mr. Thorp. May I have a few minutes of your time to get a statement from you about what happened yesterday with Mr. Jenkins?"

"Right now?" Don asked with a forced smile on his face.

"It'll only take a minute, please, sir."

John said to Don, "And while I'm here, I thought you'd like to know Larry was already terminated this mornin', so Corporal Rhodes wasn't able to talk to him."

Don asked John, half totally thrilled—half totally panicked, "Larry's fired??"

"Yup," answered John happily, "He left about an hour ago." John acted really happy, nearly giddy, as though a giant weight had been taken off of his shoulders.

Don figured he had better acquiesce about the interview so as not to raise any suspicions and said, "Well, uh, yeah. Sure come on in." The corporal entered Don's office.

John said, "I'll leave y'all alone. See ya."

Don and Rhodes both said, "'Bye," to John as he walked away.

The corporal grabbed a chair that was against one of the walls in Don's office and pulled it over to sit next to Don's desk. The very same side of the desk with the drawer where the gun had previously been. Though in Don's head, it was STILL THERE.

"Mind if I sit here?" he asked Don.

"That's fine," answered Don as he stood up to shake hands with Rhodes. "Pleased to meet you," continued Don.

"Likewise," said the corporal. "Have a seat," he said as he motioned for Don to retake his seat. Don did so.

Rhodes sat down right next to the drawer as Don nervously looked at the drawer and then quickly back at the corporal and smiled. The corporal took out a notepad from his breast pocket, opened it up and rested his arm on the desktop as Don tried to suppress a panic attack. He was doing everything he could not to hyperventilate.

"So, Mr. Jenkins' boss was telling me that there were two separate incidents between you and Jenkins yesterday?"

"Oh, uh, yeah. Two." Don nodded, yes, and stalled out there, saying nothing further.

Expecting more from someone that had been the victim of an attempted murder, twice, by the same individual, Rhodes wasn't quite understanding Don's body language and demeanor but continued anyway without addressing it. Don still hadn't said anything else, so the corporal prompted him. "So... Can you please tell me about the two incidents?" He was thinking Don's behavior was particularly odd, though he had no idea why. Normally, someone in these circumstances would be very forthcoming with information. This was like pulling teeth, he thought.

Don started off, "Well, uh, first he dropped a really big wrench from about thirty feet up at a refinery construction job. It just missed me. That thing probably weighed twenty pounds."

Rhodes was writing all of this down.

Don continued, "Then, after that, on the way back from that same construction site..."

Suddenly, Rick, Don's drafting coworker from the office next door, short, nerdy and in his late twenties, popped his head in the doorway, interrupted the interview and said to Don, "I need to use the AutoCAD manual. Louis said you have it." Don absentmindedly started to reach toward the drawer to get, THE manuals in THE drawer that were covering up THE gun, realized just what the hell he was doing and stopped before his hand was on the handle.

Don asked Rick pleadingly, "Do you have to have it right now?" trying his best to contain himself and not scream and run out the door, knocking Rick out of his way. Had Don only known, he would have gladly opened the drawer without hesitation or reservation right in front of Rhodes. No problem...

Rick said, "Well, yeah, I really need it for some codes that are in it. I'm having problems on this project and it has to be done by the end of the day," he said insistently.

"I'll get it for you when I'm done here," Don stated.

"But I need it now," Rick implored.

Rhodes piped up and said to Don, "That's OK. I can wait a minute."

Don said, "No. No. I'll, I'll get it shortly. When we're done here."

Rhodes said, "No. Really. I can wait. Been on patrol all morning and this is a break for me," he said smiling.

"No. Really. That's OK," Don said to Rhodes, then turned

236

to Rick and said assertively, "I'll get it for you in a moment. Please."

With that, Rick gave up and said, "OK," as he walked off miffed.

Rhodes said, "I'm sorry——You seem rather on edge," and then asked, "Are you OK?"

"Oh, uh, yeah, yeah. It's——It's just all the stress from Larry and not knowing if I still had a job or not..."

He nodded sympathetically to Don, "I understand... So you were saying that something else happened to you on your way back from, I think, you said a construction site?"

"Yeah," Don said. "He tried to run me off the road and then tried to deliberately have a head-on collision with me."

"Wow," said Rhodes, "This guy sounds like a serious nut case. At least he's gone from here."

"Well, that's just the thing," Don said, "He's always threatened me and my girlfriend here. Others, too. We've never felt safe because he was always threatening all of us here that he'd shoot us with his gun. He laughed about it."

"Well, maybe it's all some demented joke on his part just to rile everyone up."

Don thought, *Can't I get anyone to take this seriously?*

Rhodes asked, "So there's a history between you and him?"

"Yeah. For a long time. Years now, ever since he started working here." Then, while the corporal was there, Don wanted to see what the police response to Larry's extreme threats actually would be. Don said of Larry, "He says he really does own a gun. The way he acts and with what he's said, I know he's going to come back here and carry out his threats against us, especially now that he's been fired," said Don. Then he asked, "What can you guys do to stop him?" Don got what he expected as an answer from Rhodes.

Rhodes said, "That's just it. They're just threats at the moment. We really can't do anything unless and until he comes back and actually tries something. We'll increase our patrols in the area, but that's about all we can do. You can go to court and get a restraining order or an order of protection against him, but he really doesn't sound like the type that'll actually abide by the terms of it," then he added, "He'd probably violate it anyway."

Things like that, restraining orders and the like, are merely thin pieces of paper that offer very little, if any, real protection. No more than the thickness of the paper itself, when held up in defense as a shield, would stop a bullet. Nope. That's about what they're worth——nothing.

Rhodes said, "If something does go down, just give 911 a call and with the increased patrols, we'll be right here."

*Yeah*, Don thought, *You'll be* RIGHT HERE *five minutes after we're* ALL DEAD.

Frustrated by his lame response, Don asked, "So there's nothing you can do even though he did try to kill me a couple of times yesterday?"

The corporal said, "Unless you have some video of these two incidents, it's your word against his. I'm sure he'd just deny it—And I'm not saying it didn't happen—I believe you. But still with no evidence—what can I do?"

Don nodded understandingly but was still nonetheless nonplussed with the answer he received.

Rhodes asked, "Does your company have an armed guard here?"

"We have a guard, but he's unarmed."

"Really?" The corporal was surprised by this. He continued, "You'd think with all of his threats they'd treat this a little more seriously."

"That's the genius of our management here I guess," confided Don sarcastically.

Brandon rolled up with the mail cart in the hallway, took Don's mail out of his room's folder and started to enter the room right as Don looked at him coming through the door. Don had a kind of odd, big eyed, unnormal look about him.

Without having seen Rhodes yet, Brandon said to Don, "Hey, Holm—" Brandon's mouth froze in mid greeting and his eyes grew wide at the sight of a policeman sitting in Don's office, and right by where Brandon thought the gun was. Brandon continued his salutation a split second later, "—Holmes," trying to not look like a blow-it. Now Brandon knew why Don had a strange look on his face when he entered his office. "Here's your mail," as he handed it to Don.

"Thanks," said Don but his eyes spoke so much more...

Rhodes said, "Hi," to Brandon.

Brandon somewhat apprehensively responded, "Hey." Then he said to Don, "Well, gotta go," and exited the room quickly. He nervously rolled his cart away, thinking to himself,

*What the fuck was a cop doing in Don's office? Shit!... Did Don say anything to that cop about me? Is the cop here because of the gun? What does he know about it?* He rolled a little farther, *I'd better wait for Don to tell me what's going on... I shouldn't contact him. Maybe they're watching me and him? Shit!*

Of course Brandon had no way of knowing that the police were here about Larry's actions at the behest of John and not Brandon's and Don's actions in obtaining an illegal weapon. He naturally assumed the worst. Their defensive gunpowder gambit hadn't been discovered by anyone——other than Maggie and Michelle.

Back in Don's office, Rhodes closed up his note pad and placed it back into his pocket. He nodded his head and said, "OK. Well, I think I have all I need for now. I'll let you guy's get back to work. If there're any other questions, I'll give ya a call ——Here's one of my cards," as he fished it out of his pocket and handed it to Don. Rhodes stood up and Don did as well and they shook hands again. "Thanks for your time, Mr. Thorp. Oh, and, did you find out if you still have a job?"

"Yeah. I'm still employed."

Rhodes smiled and said, "Good for you."

Don replied, "Thanks. And thanks also for coming by. Well, have a good one..." as Don smiled because——IT WAS OVER!

"You too," responded the corporal and he walked out of the room.

Once Rhodes was out the door, Don plopped down in his chair and looked like a deflating balloon. Seconds later, Rick popped his head in the door and asked once more, "Can I get that manual, now?" which made Don almost jump right out of his skin.

After Don recovered he said, "Ah, yeah." He opened the drawer to get it out and was so happy that his meeting with the police didn't result in him being marched off to jail, he didn't even notice the gun wasn't there under the second manual. He gave the top most copy to Rick. "Here it is."

"Thanks," said Rick who hurriedly left to finish his task.

Brandon hung around the area and was still down the hall observing the situation. Once he saw the officer leaving, *without Don in handcuffs,* he headed back toward Don's office and entered it shortly after Rick left with the manual. Don looked up from his desk as he entered. Brandon's curiosity had gotten the better of him and he abandoned his plan to avoid Don in case they were being surveilled. Brandon went over by Don and whispered, "Is everything OK?"

Don said quietly back, "John called the police about what Larry tried to do to me yesterday. He was just here getting a statement from me."

Very relieved, Brandon said, "Oh. That was scary."

"Scared the hell outta me, too," Don replied. "I looked up at the door and saw a cop standing there!" Then he told Brandon, "While he was here I asked him what could be done if Larry comes back here and he said, 'Just call 911!'"

"Yeah. A lotta good that'll do us."

"No kiddin'—Oh, and Larry *was* fired today."

Brandon said, "Oh! OK. Gotta go."

Don nodded, yes, and waved 'bye at him as he exited his room. Then, Don realized that Maggie probably doesn't know, but really does need to know, that Larry *was* fired. He picked up the phone and dialed her extension.

Maggie saw it was Don on the caller ID. She hesitated to answer it fearing he'd discovered the gun missing and put two and two together. She decided not to answer it and let it go to her voice mail.

He heard her outgoing message, waited for the beep and then said, "I just wanted to let you know that John told me they did shit-can Larry today. He said Larry threatened him before he left I guess. What a shock. Anyway, I wanted you to know..." Then he added, "I love you, Maggie———'Bye." Don hung up and sat back in his chair and stared at Maggie's photograph on his desk.

In Maggie's office, after Don hung up, she saw the message light come on and opted not to find out what the message he left was about for the same reason she didn't answer in the first place. She just sat there and stared at the blinking light on her phone.


A thick marine layer of clouds had moved in from the ocean coloring everything charcoal gray at Hunter. As Rhodes' police car pulled out into the street, leaving, he passed right by Larry heading the other way toward the business concern. Larry entered his former employer's front parking lot and parked in one of the spaces facing the structure, ironically two spaces away from Slater's truck. He turned off the motor.

In his car, Larry sat and stared at the building for a couple of minutes imagining the helter-skelter chaos he was about to unleash on his prospective victims. His once and for all revenge thrilled him to the bone. He had visions of them begging for their lives as he drilled them with hot lead. A flamethrower of death and destruction.

Larry then withdrew the unloaded .45-caliber from the box, released the safety, pulled back the breach to rack the gun, aimed it out the windshield at the office building and pulled the trigger——Click. Larry chuckled.

In the lobby, simultaneous to this, Jennifer answered the reception phone. "Good morning, Hunter Engineering. How may I direct your call?... I'm sorry, Mr. Jenkins is no longer here."

Larry looked out through the windshield at the office building and then down at the gun in his lap. First, he put the safety back on so he didn't shoot himself out in the parking lot, thus ruining his plans. Next, with murderous intent, he removed the magazine from the gun and began loading it with bullets. One-by-one. A bullet for all comers, or, in this case, all goners ——or the dearly departed.

Having completed his notifications of employment, and after recovering from his confrontation with Larry, John stood in front of his computer in his office. He pushed in a thumb drive with one hand and gulped coffee from a mug with the other. He looked over at a photo of his wife and him at their daughter's wedding a few years ago. Both were all smiles in the image——as they always had been together. He couldn't wait for their vacation/second honeymoon to begin. They had never been to Hawaii. When they had first gotten married they barely had a pot to piss in, let alone tickets to a remote, exotic destination. So, the original honeymoon back then was——Niagara Falls.


Larry finished loading the first magazine and shoved it into the gun's grip with a vengeance coupled with unmitigated hate. He set the loaded gun on the passenger seat then started loading another magazine. With every projectile, another life extinguished. He didn't care. That would be his prize! Larry pictured himself in action carrying out his executions, watching himself with exhilaration as he gave it to them good.

He would start on the third floor with John, then go down to the second floor to get Maggie and Michelle, and then, the piece de resistance on the first floor——Don——and any other unfortunate targets of opportunity that he had past run-ins with. Too bad, he thought, that he couldn't find them all in the same room at the same time. John's birthday party would have been the ideal time had Larry been prepared, and his final justification had occurred. Larry's own "Final Solution" for his fellow employees. A thoroughly zealous smile formed on Larry's face and got larger and larger every time he placed another bullet in the magazine knowing what it would produce. A simple press of the trigger. No more Don. No more Maggie. No more John. No more...

Brandon was sorting parcels at his cart in one corner of the mail-room while wearing his earbuds as always and was rocking to the beat of his blaring MP3 player. His rotund supervisor, Karen, whose pungent "feminine odor" was so bad it could knock flies off of a shit wagon from fifty feet, waddled over and handed a stack of paper to him. "These," she started to say but was cut off by Brandon...

"Hang on," he said as he pulled out his earbuds. "OK. Now I can hear you."

His porcine boss resumed, "These memos have to be delivered to every person here tomorrow."

He asked, "Just one each?" as he tried to hold his breath.

"Yes," she said, "It's only a single page. Thanks." She turned and ambled away toward her office and Brandon breathed again with great relief, though her unpleasant aroma still lingered.

Larry put more rounds into yet another magazine, the only sound being the metal to metal scrape of bullets sliding into it. Much quieter than when they emerge from the barrel on their brief, hypersonic journey, followed immediately by a puff of flaming gunpowder.

Michelle was walking in the hallway carrying some paperwork. Her pleated skirt flared as she pivoted and went through the doorway into the HR conference room.

Once inside the room she began to lay out a set of documents on the conference tables in front of every chair, in the otherwise empty, at the moment, room. She opened a box of ball point pens and placed a pen next to each set of documents.

Larry put the five loaded magazines into his jacket pockets. Two, into the left pocket, and three into the right one. Then, he left an envelope on the passenger seat. The envelope was labeled: "I HATE YOU ALL!!!!!!!!" which contained his tortured, hand written note, detailing his reasons for pursuing this nightmare scenario on his innocent former coworkers.

The end was nigh. He grasped and moved the rear view mirror to where he could see his face and took a last look at himself. Larry drew in a deep breath and let it out slowly. After that, he grabbed the gun, opened the door and got out of the car.

He stood next to the open door of his car while he released the safety on the gun and pulled back the breach allowing one round to enter the chamber. He stuck the gun into the waistband of his pants and zipped up his jacket halfway to conceal it. After that, he slammed the car door hard and walked away toward the office building.

Don sat in front of the computer in his office. He typed a command, sat back and took a bite of a glazed doughnut. The printer whirred into action. He set down the doughnut, wiped his hands on a napkin then picked up a ballpoint pen and started to write on a notepad. Partway through what he was noting, he stopped and started to think about Maggie and all that had occurred this last 24 hours. He had truly risked everything over this. His job, his freedom, and the one he loved so dearly. All because they were stuck working with Charles Manson, for all practical purposes, times ten. All Larry needed was a swastika on his forehead. Unlike, Charlie, he needed no team of followers to do his bidding. Judge, jury and undertaker, all wrapped up in one psycho package from hell. Why did Don need a weapon? None of this was *that* serious, according to Maggie. He may have lost the love of his life, but wouldn't have lost his own life if there was anything he could do about it. Don was set for action. Locked and loaded. He hadn't expected Maggie to have such a severe reaction to it all, though. Nor did he expect that the weapon would NOT be there when he REALLY needed it.

Maggie paced back and forth and kept looking at the desk drawer where the gun was hidden. The phone on her desk rang, which stopped her dead in her tracks while she stared at it. It rang again. She walked over, saw it was Michelle on the caller ID and picked it up. "Hi. It's me," said Maggie.

"Hey, it's Michelle."

Maggie collapsed into her chair. "I'm glad it's you. I was afraid it might have been Don," she said, as she had second thoughts about their scheme to rid Don of the weapon. Too late now.

"You haven't heard from him?"

"No. Not yet," Maggie said, "He's going to find out what I've done sooner or later. I shouldn't have done it. He'll never trust me again."

"Why should *you* trust *him,* again?"

An entirely accurate counter argument.

Maggie admitted, "That's true. It doesn't matter at this point, I suppose——I think it's over between him and me after all this crazy shit."

"I don't blame you a bit. He's damn lucky that we're helping him out. Anyway, don't worry. We're doing the right thing. I'll be there in about fifteen minutes and we'll take it out to my car. Sound good?"

"Yeah——There's no turning back now."

"OK. See you soon."

"'Bye," said Maggie. Maggie hung up and thought to herself, *Why am I doing this to help him anyway? It's over. Why am I risking my freedom over this? If he gets found out, he'll get whatever he deserves for doing what he's done. I can't very well take the gun back to him now. Now* I'M *stuck with it... I should never have let Michelle talk me into this crazy plot.* Maggie reached over and picked up the framed photo of Don that she'd laid face down earlier. She held it in her lap as she gazed at it nostalgically and wondered, *What has my life devolved into?*

Slater was on his rounds walking next to the rear of the building. He came to the corner and turned down the side of the structure. He instantly recognized Larry walking toward him, with a purpose, from about fifty feet away. Slater authoritatively said to Larry, "I'm sorry sir, you're going to have to leave the premises." Slater reached for his walkie-talkie as Larry pulled out the gun and stuck it in Slater's face. "Whoa!" said Slater.

"Do what you're told and you won't get hurt," said Larry sternly to him.

"Sure mister."

Larry directed, "OK now. Turn around. We're going to the back doors."

Slater turned around and Larry shoved the gun in his back. "Get moving." Slater instinctively hesitated so Larry shoved the gun harder into his back. "I said move!" Slater started moving. Larry marched him back around the corner and over to the rear entrance about two hundred fifty feet away.

Larry and Slater passed by the windows of several offices on their trek to the back entrance, and not one of the employees who's views they transited noticed. They were all too busy.

"Stop right here," instructed Larry. The two stood before the back doors. "Gimme your keys and your access badge and your radio." Slater paused again a little too long so Larry pressed the gun in his back even harder. "NOW!"

Slater complied, handing over the items one-by-one. While holding the gun on him with his right hand, Larry held the electronic access badge with his left hand against its reader next to the entrance and unlocked the back doors. Larry opened one of the doors and said, "What a stroke of luck running into you," as he rubbed it in the guard's face. With that, Larry slipped inside, making sure the door latched closed and that Slater was locked out. Larry dumped the radio and the set of keys in a garbage can and sneered at Slater through the glass doors as he stuck the access badge in his pocket.

Slater was fuming.

Larry loved it. He put the gun back into his waistband under his jacket. He turned away and started down the corridor on his mission of revenge.

Slater waited until Larry was out of sight then sprinted toward the front of the building.


Larry pressed the elevator call button and nervously flexed his hands. His breathing was shallow and rapid. He glanced to the left and then to the right, then straight ahead at the elevator doors, eyes fixed on them in case one of his targets stepped out of it when the doors opened. The elevator chimed its arrival and opened, revealing——an empty elevator car. Larry stepped inside and pressed the third floor button——and stood there, and stood there. It wasn't going fast enough for Larry so just as he took his hand out of his pocket to push the door close button, it started to do so. As the lift began to ascend, he looked up at the security camera in the corner and huffed, as though it was some sort of inadequate force field that would have no hope of restraining him in any way.

John was seated at his desk. He picked up the phone, called Akino's extension and leaned back in his chair making himself comfortable while he waited for his call to be answered. "Yeah, Akino," said John, "I need the figures for the turbine project... Excellent. See you in a minute."

Still running as fast as he could, Slater neared the front of the building.

John quickly called the number for the company with the turbine project that Hunter was designing, then swiveled his chair around to look out the window. "Hello, Mike?... This is John. I have some good news for you about the turbine project." Even though he was looking out the window, unfortunately, John was so focused on business that he was totally oblivious to the sight of the guard running to his truck full-tilt outside, three stories below.

The chime went off at the third floor elevator lobby. The doors parted and Larry stepped out. He moved quickly down the hallway toward John's office. No one else was in sight. Larry's face had broken out in a sweat and his eyes were glazed over. It was then! Finally! What he'd always dreamed of doing was really about to happen!

John was still conversing on the phone sitting in his chair with his back to the door. Behind him, Larry entered the room. John said to the person on the phone, "Yeah, they did." Larry unzipped his jacket and pulled out the gun. John heard this and began to turn his chair around expecting Akino with the data he'd requested. John continued to the person on the phone, "Hey, hang on a minute. Akino's here with the..." To his ultimate horror, John saw Larry standing there with a gun trained on him. John freaked out and dropped the phone. "Larry!! What're you doin'??!!"

"What's it look like I'm doing? I told you I'd be back."

John screamed, "NO!!"

Larry fired.

BANG!!!

John was hit right in the chest. A huge gush of blood splattered his desk.


While watering a plant in her office, Maggie gasped at the sound of the gunshot with an aghast look on her face. Quickly replaced by the realization, *Oh, no! I took the gun away from Don!*


Simultaneously, Don was on the phone in his office and looked up in shock at the sound and knew what it was immediately and said, "Larry!" His worst fears had come to fruition.

John's lifeless body was slumped to one side in the chair. His eyes were wide open, frozen in terror. Larry's smile was beyond sexual exhilaration. For good measure and just to make sure, he fired a slug into John's forehead.

BANG!!!

Don dropped the phone and frantically opened the bottom desk drawer and lifted up the second manual. The gun was missing! He tore through the rest of the items in the drawer but couldn't locate the weapon and exclaimed, "Where the fuck is it??!!" He did a cursory search of the other drawers and pounded the desk with his fist, leaped from the chair and charged out of his office. A few seconds after he exited, his phone started ringing.

Maggie stood behind her desk with the phone up to her ear and heard, "Hi. You've reached Don Thorp. Please leave a message and I'll get..." She nervously bit her lower lip.

Way down in the lobby, Jennifer heard the shots, leaped out of her seat, picked up the walkie-talkie and ran for the front doors. As she ran, she keyed the mic and asked in a panicked tone, "Eric! Are you there?! I heard what sounded like gun shots! I'm heading outside!" as she made it through the front doors with several others and ran as fast as she could away from the entrance.

In the trash can by the back door, you could hear Jennifer's continued desperate cry for help on Slater's disposed of walkie-talkie, "Eric, are you there?! Are you there?!"


Akino ran up to the doorway of John's office and saw Larry with a gun and John's dead body. With a horrified look, Akino did an instant 180 but Larry shot him in the back.

BANG!!!

The blast sent Akino careening into the opposing wall in the hallway. The paperwork he was carrying flew in all directions.

Larry emerged from John's office, stood over Akino's crumpled body and aimed at his head. A woman in the next office ran out into the hallway, saw what was happening and started screaming hysterically. Larry looked over at her and said, "Get the fuck outta here!" She fled in horror away down the hall as Larry turned his attention back to Akino laying in the hallway.


Brandon steered the mail cart down a different hallway on the same floor. He had his earbuds in and the volume cranked as usual.

BANG!!!

As the sound traveled down the hallway, Brandon was

completely unaware of the gunshot's echo due to his tunes over-whelming it. The loud report of the gun-blast caused some let-ters to fall off of the cart's outgoing tray and onto the floor. He stopped, picked them up and continued on his way.

More people were running out of the front doors and away from the building. Slater was flying toward his pick-up. From his viewpoint, the truck got closer and closer. He had heard the shots going off inside the building which spurred him on even more to help the helpless inside.

He was nearly out of breath when he reached his truck. He habitually reached for his missing keys, remembered they were confiscated by Larry, then grabbed a baseball bat from the bed of the pick-up and bashed-in the driver's side window. Sla-ter reached in, unlocked the door and opened it. Next, he quickly folded the seat forward and grabbed the 12 gauge shotgun.

Akino's body was left in a bloody heap on the floor as Larry walked away. The hysterical woman continued running and screaming. Two men ran out of an office after she flew by. They stopped and looked at Larry and Akino. The two men freaked out, then ran away right behind the woman.

Larry made no attempt to shoot them whatsoever. They weren't on his shit list.

Down the hall, Brandon's earbuds still roared with music as he pushed the mail cart and neared a turn in the hallway. Suddenly, the hysterical woman and the two freaked out men following her close behind came flying around the corner and nearly crashed into the cart.

The first man yelled at Brandon, "Run!! He's got a gun!!"

Brandon watched them run by but couldn't hear them over the music. Brandon yelled at the two men, "Get her!" as though they were chasing her. He snickered as he looked back at the woman and the men as they ducked into a stairwell. As he turned back toward the mail cart, suddenly, Brandon looked puzzled and then a flash of realization hit him hard just as Larry rounded the corner, ten feet away!

Their eyes met and Larry raised up the gun to shoot.

In a panic, Brandon flipped the mail cart up at Larry.

Larry fired.

BANG!!!

Letters flew everywhere as the bullet went right through the flimsy, no protection at all mail cart and hit Brandon square in the stomach. The impact knocked off his earbuds and hurled him into a nearby water cooler. Brandon and the cooler hit the floor in a loud splash of blood and water.

Lying helplessly on the floor face up, Brandon was barely alive, choking and gagging on blood. His knocked-off earbuds were still blaring music in an eerie, surreal juxtaposition.

Larry walked right up to, and stood over, Brandon who saw Larry's shoes and strained to look up. Brandon's last view on Earth was of Larry's towering figure and the gun pointed downward, directly at his head, just inches away. In one final gust of strength, Brandon begged for his life, "Larry... pp... please... no..."

Larry fired.

BANG!!!

Blood droplets splattered Larry's trousers.


Slater ran up to the front doors and entered them as three more people, two women and a man ran outside. One of the women yelled to Slater, "I'm so glad you're here!"


Don ran down the hallway dodging people running the opposite direction. He smacked into Louis who grabbed Don by the arm and asked, "Where the hell are you going??!" Louis attempted to stop him, but Don pulled away and ran onward toward Maggie's office. Louis gave up on Don and continued onward toward the outside with the rest of the panicked employees and visitors.


Michelle hid behind a corner in a hall on the second floor. She slowly peeked around it and saw nothing and started running as fast as she could toward the stairway exit which lead to the comparative safety of outside. She opened a door marked in large blue letters: "Stairs – 2nd Floor" and rushed through it to the stairwell inside.

At the same time, bloody footprints on the carpet lead away from Brandon's bloody demise. A few feet down the hall, Larry opened a door marked in large red letters: "Stairs – 3rd Floor."

As Michelle ran down the stairs one level below, Larry, one level above, walked down the same set of stairs, in the same stairwell, at the same time, totally unaware that one of his targets was right beneath him trying to escape the horror. Moving much faster than he, Michelle ducked out the first floor doorway a few seconds before Larry reached the second floor stairway door.

Maggie was crouched down behind her desk, trembling. She got her purse out of the bottom desk drawer, opened it, removed the gun and stared at it in her hand. She saw it in an entirely new light that she'd never seen it in before. *Don was right?? What have I done? What if he gets killed out in the hall now because of me?* she thought as she wiped tears away with the back of her free hand.

A door that was marked in big blue letters: "Stairs – 2nd Floor" slowly swung shut as Larry walked away down the hall. He tossed a spent magazine on the floor and slapped in a fresh one. The closing stairway door latched shut with a loud, ka-chunk.

Down on the first floor, Slater ran with the shotgun braced diagonally against his chest fighting a torrent of people rushing toward him. "Get out!! Now!!" he urged them all as he passed them as he ran toward the trouble, a credit to his profession and convictions.

Two women ran out of a stairwell marked in big orange letters: "Stairs – 1st Floor" and saw Slater approaching fast. They pointed upward frantically, "We just saw him up on the second floor near HR!"

He yanked the stairwell door open and flew through it.


Maggie was now hiding in the knee hole of her desk with a terrified look on her face. She had her finger on the trigger of the gun, ready for the worst, even though she was shaking so badly she could barely hold onto it.


Next to an open door in HR was a nameplate that read: "MICHELLE JEFFRIES." Larry approached rapidly and entered Michelle's vacated office with his gun raised to kill and a big smile on his face.


At the same time, Michelle opened and ran out the front doors to the outside. She got to keep her job *and* her life that day.

Larry looked in the knee hole under Michelle's desk and saw nothing. He gave the desk a hard kick in frustration. "Fucking bitch!" He headed back out into the hallway.


Now on the second floor, Slater ran full speed up to a 'T' intersection of corridors. He rounded the corner doing a "gangster turn," nearly side-swiping the wall————and there was Larry, walking right toward him about forty feet away! Slater instantly did an about face and ducked just as Larry shot from his hip.

BANG!!!

Larry's shot flew above Slater, missing him but striking a fleeing woman downrange in the shoulder. She screamed, stumbled a bit, then continued to run away.

Slater leaped behind the corner he came from as Larry fired off another round.

BANG!!!

The shot pierced the wall and rocketed through the other side, narrowly missing Slater and taking a chunk of drywall with it. Slater was very winded and looked desperate. He pumped the handle of the shotgun, racking it, which was still braced against his chest. Now there was one shell ready in the chamber. Sweat poured down his face as he tried to wipe it from his eyes and blinked to clear them a couple of times. Slater spun on his heel around the edge of the corner and fired the shotgun at Larry.

BOOM!!!

Slater ducked back behind the wall.

Larry dove through the doorway of the interior corner office Slater was hiding behind. Larry was winged by a few pieces of buckshot. He grasped at his wounded arm, his face twisted in pain. He could hear the guard rack the shotgun pump again. Larry aimed his .45-caliber at the wall, estimated Slater's position, then launched a barrage of bullets as fast as he could squeeze them off.

BANG!!! BANG!!! BANG!!! BANG!!! BANG!!!

Larry emptied the magazine as he strafed the wall left to right, leaving holes six to eight inches apart. Click, click, click, once the magazine was empty. He could hear Slater falling down.

Slater was on the floor, bleeding profusely from his torso and groping for the shotgun. He just managed to grab it and attempted to aim it upward. He could hear the sound of one of Larry's spent magazines hit the floor after Larry ejected it.

In the corner office, Larry slapped in a fresh magazine. He cautiously looked around the edge of the doorway and stepped into the hall. Larry started around the corner and Slater fired another blast with the shotgun.

BOOM!!!

The buckshot pelted the wall behind Larry, missing him completely. Slater desperately tried to pump the shotgun handle with his slippery, blood soaked hand. Larry walked right up to him, and at close range, fired into the guard's forehead.

BANG!!!

Slater's body laid there jerking briefly in postmortem tremor.

Larry resumed his trek with an ever more trance-like,

bloodthirsty look on his face. With Michelle's location unknown, all that were left on his list of revenge were Don and Maggie.

Sylvia and Petrovitch ducked out the front doors and started running away from the building toward the growing crowd of fleeing employees farther out in the front parking lot. The amorphous assemblage kept moving, wanting to put significant distance between themselves and the building that they exited like a sinking ship as the gunshots continued.

Rankin was running as fast as he could through the front parking lot when he encountered Petrovitch who yelled at him, "Get over here!! Now!!"

Rankin saw who it was, changed his direction and headed toward Petrovitch's location, very winded. Petrovitch and Sylvia were still moving away from the building, just not running any longer. Petrovitch was a little winded, too. Rankin finally reached them.

Petrovitch said angrily, "THIS was YOUR last day. This is all your Goddamn fault!"

"But, sir. I can explain and, and also that's not according to protocols..."

Petrovitch cut him off, "Protocols?! When this is over, get your things and leave here immediately! You are so fired!"

"But that's not per the protocols for..."

"Shut up you incompetent boob! People are probably dying in there because you never acted on this mad man we had working here! That's not 'per the protocols' either, is it?! Now it's too late——And it's too late for you!"


Maggie was still hiding in the knee hole of her desk. She heard someone running in the hallway toward her room. She looked at the gun in her trembling hand. From down the hallway she heard Don's voice yelling, "Maggie!!"

She couldn't believe it! "Don, it's you!!" Tears welled up in her eyes once more. She quickly slid out from under the desk and stood up holding the gun at her side.


Several feet away, down a turn in the hallway, Larry heard Don and Maggie's voices and smiled maniacally. He thought, *Perfect! They're both together in one place and can watch each other die!* He rounded the corner of the hallway he was in just in time to see Don nearing Maggie's office.

Don got to her doorway and saw Maggie with the gun. "You've got it!" Don headed for Maggie.

"Oh, Don. I was afraid you might be dead!"

"C'mon! Let's get the hell out of here," he strongly suggested. Just as Don reached Maggie on the other side of her desk, Larry showed up in her doorway. Larry aimed his gun toward Don as Maggie raised her gun holding it with both hands, cocked the hammer and instinctually took aim at Larry as she trembled.

Larry was startled by her weapon and actually froze. That was something he hadn't counted on. An armed response from them!

Maggie hesitated.

Don implored, "Shoot him!!"

Larry fired wild first.

BANG!!!

The bullet zipped right between Don and Maggie, striking the wall behind them in a puff of plaster.

Maggie returned fire.

BOOM!!!

The hefty bullet hit Larry square in the left elbow, completely severing his forearm causing it to fly across the hall. The force of the blast sent him reeling around, spun counterclockwise like a pinwheel, with his back slammed against the wall in the hallway outside her office.

Maggie shrieked and dropped behind her desk. Don ducked behind the desk with her. Panicked, she handed the gun to him.

Larry stood there in the hallway, still with his back against the wall, dazed and in shock. He looked down at the blood pouring from where his left arm used to be. Then he looked over at his severed arm lying a few feet away.

Don and Maggie strained to listen for any sound they could hear above the loud ringing in their ears.

Larry looked like he was fading fast. He eased himself down to a sitting position on the floor with his legs stretched out in front of him. Excruciating pain contorted his face. "Fuckers!" He looked down at the gun in his hand and then looked straight ahead. He stuck the gun barrel in his mouth, and without any hesitation, pulled the trigger.

BANG!!!

Larry blew his brains out of the back of his skull. The gun went spinning across the floor as Larry slumped to one side. On the wall above Larry was a corny looking poster, now splattered with blood, titled: "Workplace Safety."

*Finally*, the sound of police sirens could be heard approaching in the distance.

With the gun raised and ready, Don stood back up, slowly and quietly, made his way over to the doorway and cautiously looked out.

Maggie asked hysterically, "Did I kill him?! Is he dead?!"

Don saw Larry motionless, slumped over on the floor——minus the back of his head.

Maggie peeked over her desk.

Don looked back at her, "I think he killed himself."

Maggie stood up as Don rushed over to her. He laid the gun on her desk and took her in his arms. They held each other tightly.

"It's over now," he comforted her, "We don't have to worry about him ever again." Tears ran down her cheeks. Still in each other's arms, Don pulled back so that they were face to face. He continued, "We're both still alive and that's all I ever wanted." They had no idea about the fate of their two best friends, Brandon and Michelle. They only knew for certain that they, themselves, had survived this hideous ordeal.

"Oh, Don, what's going to happen to us now?"

After a moment he responded, "We'll have to talk to the

police. All we can do is tell them exactly what happened——We probably won't have jobs anymore. And, hopefully I won't be arrested over the thing that saved our lives."

Maggie said, "But we'll still have each other——I love you, Don."

"I love you, Maggie. More than anything else in the world." After a few seconds further to compose themselves, he said, "C'mon, let's get outta here. And—don't look at him on the way out."

She nodded, yes, and leaned on him. He put his arm around her and slowly lead her away to the sound of many more sirens approaching their building from all directions——having left the revolver behind on her desktop.

▪ – — —*Thank You for Reading My Writings* — — – ▪

Cover Design: Mark J. Wilson
Cover Artwork ©2020 Mark J. Wilson/Actis Productions

Mark J. Wilson has worked in the field of motion pictures and video
for nearly 30 years. He variously produces, directs, writes,
photographs and edits. His credits include: "Pop Kowboy"
"Bubba And Sissy Git Hitched?" and "Disposable."
He is on the IMDb.com as Mark J. Wilson producer of "Time Bomb."

markjwilson.author@gmail.com